OFF WE GO INTO THE WILD BLUE YONDER

OFF WE GO INTO THE WILD BLUE YONDER

A NOVEL BY TRAVIS NICHOLS

COFFEE HOUSE PRESS

MINNEAPOLIS

2010

Coffee House Press books are available to the trade through our primary distributor, Consortium Book Sales & Distribution, www.cbsd.com or (800) 283-3572. For personal orders, catalogs, or other information, write to: info@coffeehousepress.org.

Coffee House Press is a nonprofit literary publishing house. Support from private foundations, corporate giving programs, government programs, and generous individuals helps make the publication of our books possible. We gratefully acknowledge their support in detail in the back of this book. To you and our many readers around the world, we send our thanks for your continuing support.

Good books are brewing at coffeehousepress.org

LIBRARY OF CONGRESS CATALOGING-IN-PUBLICATION DATA

Nichols, Travis, 1979–
Off we go into the wild blue yonder / Travis Nichols.
p. cm.
ISBN 978-1-56689-241-4 (alk. paper)
1. Grandfathers—Fiction. 2. Grandsons—Fiction. 3. World War, 1939–1945—Veterans—Fiction. 4. World War, 1939–1945—Aerial operations, American—Fiction. 5. Airmen—United States—Fiction. 6. Americans—Poland—Fiction. 7. Reminiscing in old age—Fiction. 8. Voyages and travels—Fiction. I. Title.
PS3614.I3532O37 2010
813'.6—DC22
2010000381

PRINTED IN CANADA
FIRST EDITION | FIRST PRINTING
1 3 5 7 9 8 6 4 2

ACKNOWLEDGMENTS

Excerpts from this work appeared previously in *Denver Quarterly* and *Filter*. The author wishes to thank the editors of those publications, as well as Monica Fambrough, Joshua Beckman, Noah Eli Gordon, Paul Killebrew, Anna Myczkowska, Tomaž Šalamun, Laura Solomon, and Robert Underhill for their invaluable love and support.

Lyrics reprinted from "The Air Force Song," by Robert Crawford.

For my family.

Dear Luddie,

I don't remember much about the first thing I killed, but I remember I killed it with a knife. I cut it open with a knife and said, "I want the guts! I want the guts! I want the guts! I want the guts!" My older brother turned green beside me. It was a fish. The knife I killed it with had a white handle. The white handle had small, blue marks on it.

My brother and I had been fishing in a pond by the Bombardier's house. Cows and dogs strolled by with their different tongues while we stood in the grass with our lines in the water. Neither of us had ever caught a fish before. We had fished and fished and caught nothing but water. But I caught that fish, and when I caught it, I didn't look at it, hold it, or study it. I just cut it open.

There is nothing in my mind now about the fish—what it looked like, what it felt like, or what it smelled like—there is only the knife, and my brother turning green, and me saying, "I want the guts!" over and over again.

Since that fish, I've killed a few other fish, plenty of flies, moths, beetles, worms, hermit crabs, fireflies, and a mouse.

No people.

I haven't killed any people, Luddie, but it's true I have come close. I've come close by holding my step-dad's gun to my brother's temple and pulling the trigger.

I was just a kid then, curious and alone and with my brother who was curious and alone too.

I didn't know if the chamber held a bullet and I didn't know what it would mean if it did, but I pulled the trigger. "On or off?" I said to my brother and then I pulled the trigger before he could answer.

Nothing happened.

"On," I said.

And then I put the barrel to my own temple, and I squeezed the little metal tongue to prove there was nothing. Nothing at all.

"On or off?" I said again, and again the hollow click sounded.

"On," I said.

Would it have been better off? To light up my eyes from inside, to feel my little brains go black?

They didn't.

My brother punched me in the head and called me a word I didn't know, and my brains didn't go black at all.

My brains didn't go black at all, and my brother and I lived, and later that same year we killed other things with pleasure.

Ants, mice, spiders, fish. A swarm of horseflies had filled our room.

I remember the room was dark and heavy with flies and we swatted them out of the air with flyswatters. Giddy with killing, we swatted them so hard they splattered against the walls and the ceiling, and by the time the horseflies stopped flying around the room, black and red smudges covered the walls and the ceiling, and sweat poured off of my brother and me.

We turned all the flies off in wet splats and bursts.

Another time, my brother and I walked up and down the beach, taking turns hitting hermit crabs into the ocean with a piece of driftwood.

When it was my turn, my brother tossed a hermit crab into the air and I swung the driftwood stick, smashing the shell, sending its pieces one way and the little crab hurtling out over the ocean the other way.

I remember one of those crabs' claws frantically scratching at the sky after I hit it with the stick. I'm sure I killed that one, Luddie, and I remember it didn't seem to want to die.

Dear Luddie,

Maybe I'm forgetting something. Maybe I'm forgetting something I've killed, or something that has died and taken part of my story with it.

It's a mystery, like waking up in the middle of the night and saying something deadly to the person in bed with you and then falling back to sleep.

In the morning, when the person in bed with you tells you the deadly thing you said, you know the deadly thing, but you don't remember saying it. Your story has become confused, but you don't know how. You don't know how because you don't remember saying that deadly thing, a thing you would never say to anyone. All you remember is the sleep, the black wool of it, and because that is all you remember, your story becomes confused.

I don't want my story to become confused, Luddie.

I want my story to be clear, so I think I need to push past the black wool of sleep.

I need to push past the black wool of sleep and I need to remember the deadly things, both the said and the unsaid, but I'm not sure how to do it.

It might help, I think, if you write back and tell me what you remember about what you've killed.

It might help, I think, if you write back and tell me what you remember about what you've lived through.

Dear Luddie,

In my dream, I am in the sky with the Bombardier. The earth has sent yellow ropes into the sky, and these ropes have reached through the clouds and circled our insides.

These ropes pull us down by our insides.

When the ropes return to earth, I know they will have metal, cloth, and bodies with them. When the ropes return to earth, I will let small animals lick the clouds from my arms and my legs and my spilled insides. But for now, in my dream, all is anticipation and rushing sky.

We're falling. The Bombardier and I.

In the rushing sky, the Bombardier turns to me and screams, "Where is the enemy?"

I don't recognize this Bombardier who turns to me and screams, Luddie, and I don't know where the enemy is.

I am terrified.

It is 1944.

We're falling.

When I wake up from this dream, I feel wet black wool between my bones and muscle. I feel it in my sinuses and lungs. It leaves me clouded in my bed, as if I haven't fully fallen out of the sky, or as if I haven't fully fallen out of the dream, as if I'm still in the sky with the ropes around my insides.

I'm telling you, Luddie, because I want to know if you are in this dream, if you see the Bombardier turning to me, screaming, or if you ever dream the same dream. If I turn to you in your dream, or if you dream at all.

Please write.

Dear Luddie,

I know my story, and I could tell it to you, but my story is less important than the Bombardier's story. The Bombardier isn't only in my dream but in real life too. You know this. He has a story. I know some of his story, and you know some of his story too, so maybe we should tell each other what we know.

Yes?

In time, will you tell me what you know?

Okay, then I will tell you what I know. I will tell the story that I know.

I know that the Bombardier was born in the Midwest. He was born in the Midwest between the wars. This is his story. He was born in the Midwest to a woman in a blue dress and a man with red hair. Between the wars, this man and this woman had three other boys in the house with the Bombardier, and the mother in the blue dress cooked and the man with red hair drank himself down the railroad line, away from the cooking, the blue dress, the house, the brothers, and the Bombardier.

Do you know this?

Do you know that away from their red-haired father, the brothers grew up and played baseball in fields of dead prairie grass in the Midwest? That none of them had red hair like their father, and that suited them fine?

"Have you seen him?" one brother asked the other.

"Nope," the other brother said, pushing a rock in the dirt with a stick.

"Hmm," said another brother.

The Bombardier hopped onto a rusted Buick that sat in the tall grass.

"Who wants a ride?" he asked his brothers.

He didn't know how to drive.

No one had taught him.

His father used to drive the Buick, but now his father was gone, and when he rode in the back of the Buick now he got sick from the swaying, so he always begged to stay home.

He shifted the gears and honked the horn in the grass. If he could drive the Buick, he thought, then he might not get sick.

I know this because the Bombardier himself told me, while teaching me how to drive and how to play baseball in dead fields in the Midwest. This is his story.

I know that some days in his story, the Bombardier went to school in the Midwest, between the wars, and other days he stayed home. I know he liked school, and he liked to read, so he went to school when he couldn't play baseball, when he didn't have chores to do.

I know in school he read Plato and then he read Aristotle.

I like to imagine that when he read Plato and when he read Aristotle, his brain felt like it had little arms and little legs. When he read, it felt like his brain flew with its little arms and little legs pointed straight out in the air against a strong, cold wind. I like to imagine the Bombardier liked the feeling.

I like to imagine that though he liked the feeling, he didn't know where his flying brain could go, so when he graduated from high school in the Midwest—it wasn't so hard—he became the easiest thing for him to become.

He became a salesman.

I know he sold shoes and he sold lots of them, so soon he left the Midwest and traveled down to the Southwest and up to New England selling, selling, selling.

If his brain couldn't fly by itself at least the rest of his body could take his brain along with it.

His body and his brain had traveled to a hotel in Arizona on December

7, 1941, and on December 8, 1941, he turned the radio on in his hotel there in Arizona.

The sound bounced off the bubbled wallpaper and the yellow lamp cord.

The radio in his hotel told the Bombardier that the Japanese had attacked America. The frenzied voices bounced off of the bubbled wallpaper and the yellow lamp cord and the Bombardier heard them.

Pearl Harbor had happened and the Bombardier heard about it over the radio.

On December 8, 1941, the Bombardier listened to the radio and put the last of his sample shoes into the corner of his paper suitcase. He shut his paper suitcase, and he put his hands on his knees. He went down to the lobby and picked up the black phone on the counter to call the airline. He asked the airline for a flight back home to the Midwest. He would stop selling shoes and join the armed services.

He was ready to fight, so he knew, in the Midwest or in the Southwest or in New England, he would join the armed services and go fight the Japanese and the Germans and the Italians, and that his three brothers would fight them too.

He was twenty-two.

I know they all have stories to tell, all the brothers, but they haven't told them to me, so I don't know what to tell you about them, Luddie. The Bombardier has told me his story, so I know it, and I know I am a part of it.

If you let me, I will tell the rest of the Bombardier's story to you, Luddie, though I don't know what of it you already know, or what of it is you. I don't even know where you are, Luddie, or where I could send this story to, but I believe I will find out soon enough, so I'm writing and writing to you. Please.

Dear Luddie,

I know it's tempting to say two babies were born in 1944, two years later, well into the war, the bombs, the sky.

I know it's tempting to say one baby lived while the other baby died.

Even more tempting is to say both babies were born at the same time, on the same day, December 26, 1944, the day after that year's Christians celebrated the birth of the man who died for their sins.

It's tempting I know, but I think this temptation should be resisted for a truth more ordinary, that on that day, December 26, 1944, there were two United States airmen among many bombing the Nazi-filled fields in Eastern and Central Europe, and like any other day, two babies were born among many. Some of these babies lived and some of these babies died.

Some of the many United States airmen bombing Europe that day survived and returned to America. They got married to American girls and had American babies with those girls. As often happens, those American babies had other American babies, some of which lived and some of which died.

The American babies that lived are now old enough to have their own American babies, though some of these old-enough American babies haven't yet had their own babies, but they will, and some of them will live and some of them will die.

Some of the new babies will live to be the Bombardier's great-grand-babies, because he was one of the United States airmen who lived to go home and have babies. Some of the other ones did not live, or have any babies, or tell their stories to me, a grandbaby, or to you, Luddie.

Dear Luddie,
Did you see any bombs on that day?

Dear Luddie,
Do you have any babies?

Dear Luddie,

I want to tell you the story of what happens to me, and I want you to understand, but I realize I know almost nothing about you except your name, and telling a story to someone you don't know is like praying to a God you don't understand.

I want to understand, Luddie.

I have seen a small black-and-white photograph with your name and your street written in black ink on the white backing, but I don't recognize the handwriting.

Maybe the handwriting is yours.

Maybe the photograph is of you.

In this photograph, you have black eyes and black hair, black dimples, a black dress, and black shadows under the white pearls around your white neck. You have white teeth and white skin. There is a soft, white light shining on you because it's a portrait, staged, yet you look natural, warm, motherly, like a miniature white mammal in a black velvet box.

I like to think that it is your street on the white backing, that it is your black handwriting.

What happens to me will happen in a few days, when Bernadette and I will fly from New England to meet the Bombardier in Chicago.

We're flying from New England to Chicago to give the Bombardier a present.

The present is a journey to Germany and then to Poland to see what, in 1944, was a dead field just outside Nazi territory, but now, in 2004, will surely be something else.

We are going to find something there in this present, Luddie, and I'm going to tell you all about it.

I'm going to tell you about it in these letters, and I'm going to tell you about it even if I never find you. I'm going to tell you about it even if you never write me back to tell me about your bombs or your babies.

Dear Luddie,

I have a strange story I want to tell you.

I want to tell you this strange story before anything happens to me.

It is a strange story called "How I Want to Be 'Madame Psychosis.'"

I'm going to tell you this strange story about wanting to be "Madame Psychosis" so if you don't want to know it just close your eyes and wait for the letter to be over, okay?

Okay.

Here it goes.

One night when I was nineteen, I walked around the side streets of a city. I was on drugs, in the rain, amongst chimerical corridors I saw in every direction.

Down one chimerical corridor I ran my hands along a rainy wall and found a loose doorknob.

I pulled on it.

Already that night, I had seen a little man in a black-and-white suit tapping his hobnailed boot on a linoleum floor. I had seen a Mexican man with swirling round eyes telling me he had been evicted from the Garden of Eden. I had seen huge koi fish swimming up the walls of my brother's apartment into a red pool, and I had seen my own brain bleeding black on his hardwood floor.

The doorknob came off in my hand.

When the doorknob came off in my hand, something weird and white flashed up my arm, through my chest, and into my head.

This weird white thing scared me so badly I put the doorknob in the pocket of my army jacket and ran back to my brother's apartment, singing as loud as I could.

I sang and sang.

By the time I got to his apartment I wasn't singing but screaming and scaring everyone.

It sounds stupid now, Luddie, as I'm telling it, but then, when I was nineteen years old, on drugs that were supposed to make everything in the universe connect with me but instead made everything in the universe pursue me, I felt like I touched a ghost through that doorknob, or, that a ghost touched me.

My ghost.

That night, when it didn't sound so stupid, I told my brother about my ghost touching me through the doorknob. He took the doorknob from my trembling hand, and he put it in his fist. He put it in his fist and he punched me in the mouth with the doorknob in his fist.

The ghost filled me then and I fell on the floor full of weird white and trembling.

My brother looked down at me with crazy, drug-filled eyes and red hair and he laughed. He looked down at me on the floor and he said the doorknob had now been baptized.

It needed a new name.

My brother kissed the doorknob in his hand and said, "I dub thee 'Madame Psychosis' and I deposit thee into this pocket and I renounce thee."

He leaned down to me and dropped the doorknob in my pocket.

And then he laughed.

The rest of the night, so I could forget my correspondence with the ghost, my brother and I plunged into ritualistic drug adventures.

We wrote songs on the typewriter and covered each other with shaving cream.

I thought I might slip into insanity if I didn't forget my correspondence with the ghost, and so I made myself forget, and by the time I got back to my own cinderblock apartment on a small hill at six in the morning, I was singing again.

There, I made coffee and tried to compose myself enough to go to work, but when I looked in the mirror I saw my mouth. My swollen, purple mouth. I saw my swollen, purple mouth, and I put my hand in my pocket, and I remembered. The cinderblock walls disappeared. My weird white ghost filled me again, and I fell to the floor, screaming.

I was so scared by this weird white ghost, Luddie, because I thought it was the dead me.

I threw the doorknob against the wall and shrieked.

I went a little crazy.

But I'm better now because I know that a ghost doesn't have to be dead. I know now a ghost is only something not in the present. I know now that in the present, a person is made flesh, but one second into the past or one second into the future, that flesh is gone. The person of that time—past or future—is only an idea. Only an echo, a memory, or a ghost.

There are books about this, Luddie. I'm not making it up.

I know now that it wasn't the ghost of the dead twenty-four-year-old me that grabbed my hand around the doorknob, but the ghost of the alive twenty-four-year-old me that grabbed my hand.

He might have been dreaming, or listening to a song, or staring out the window on the bus. It doesn't really matter. What matters is through the doorknob, through "Madame Psychosis," this ghost from another time corresponded with me.

What matters is that on this trip, Luddie, with Bernadette and the Bombardier, I want to be like that doorknob. I want to be the thing through which the real, present, fleshy Bombardier communicates with his ghost, to show his ghost that he'll make it to be eighty-four years old, that the enemy won't get him, that his babies won't die.

Time is not a line, Luddie. It's not a circle either, but something geometry doesn't understand.

Geometry doesn't understand it, and neither do I, Luddie, but I know that I want to be the correspondent between the past and the present.

I want to be "Madame Psychosis."

Please help me.

Dear Luddie,

Something has happened to me, but it is not what I thought would happen to me when I told you something was going to happen to me.

Something has happened to me because I left New England and came back to the Midwest, where I was born.

I should have known better than to come back to where I was born because time is not a circle.

Is it a line?

I should have known better because it's always dangerous to come back, especially if you leave from a new home to come back to where you were born. It's always dangerous because if you give where you were born a chance, it will wrap its roots around your insides and pull you down close to its ground.

This might sound pleasant or sweet, but it is neither pleasant nor sweet.

It's terrible.

Especially in the Midwest.

When the Midwest wraps its roots around your insides, the Midwest has you, and it will not let you go until you die. Unless you die there, in the Midwest, you must fight the Midwest like you have to fight an evil sleep in a black forest full of wolves.

You should never come to the Midwest, Luddie. You should never come to the Midwest unless you have to, and if you have to, you should only stay for a minute so the Midwest will not be able to wrap its roots around any of your insides, your heart, your brain, or your spleen. The Midwest is a strange enemy, Luddie, but it is an enemy. Ask anyone here. They'll tell you.

Dear Luddie,

What I thought would happen was that we would come to the Midwest for only a minute. We would come to the Midwest for only a minute, get the Bombardier, and fly off to Germany with him. That is what I thought would happen, but we weren't quick enough, and so the brown and black roots tied our insides and pulled us down. They pulled us down to what now passes for ground here in the Midwest but is actually thin green carpet over concrete.

What I thought would happen: we would come to the Midwest and meet the Bombardier in the Midwest. We would then leave all together in a quick minute for Germany. But when we came to the Midwest, the Bombardier wasn't where he should have been, so we stayed longer than a minute looking for him. We stayed longer than a minute looking for him and we didn't find him, and now I fear we will be here the rest of our lives until we die of boredom or suffocation or sleep.

This place has its own laws of physics, Luddie, its own laws of gravity, its own laws of light, its own laws of evaporation. It's like a weird, grassy moon of Jupiter.

It's no use trying to fully understand these laws in this enemy territory, this weird moon Midwest. You can only understand that these laws will pull you down and hold you there until the grass towers above your head like a dead city of dark green spires. They will hold you down until you die.

Dear Luddie,

We waited for the Bombardier with the present we had to give: a journey to Germany and then to Poland. We waited for him with the present because a woman in a blue suit told us to wait for him. She told us if we waited for him he might appear and we might still give him the present and leave for Germany and then for Poland together as we planned under the laws of New England. We planned under the laws of New England but as we waited we felt the laws of New England leave us and the laws of the evil moon Midwest press down on our shoulders and slither up our knees.

As we sat with these laws slithering around us, we listened to the woman in the blue suit and we believed her because we had nothing else to do. We stayed in Chicago with weird moon laws pressing on our shoulders and black brown roots tied to our insides, and we did what the captives of the evil moon Midwest do.

We ate some chewy nachos at the airport bar, and we waited.

Dear Luddie,

Some people do not understand what I mean when I say "we."

When I say "we," some people, like my brother, do not understand what it means.

On the phone with my brother, I said, "We are going to meet in Chicago to fly to Germany," and he was silent.

I said, "From Germany we are going to drive to Poland," and he was silent for a second time, but then when I said, "We are going to help the Bombardier find Luddie," my brother said, "What do you mean when you say 'we'?"

I hung up on him. He didn't understand at all what I meant.

What I meant is me and Bernadette.

What I mean is that Bernadette and I have to go.

If we don't go, nothing will correspond, and the Bombardier will never get his present. What I mean is correspondence must have ghosts, but it must also have witnesses and relief and doorknobs.

Do you understand, Luddie, what I mean?

Bernadette understands, and the Bombardier understands, and I understand, but my brother does not understand, and so he is not coming with us.

I hope you understand, Luddie, and that we will all—ghost, Bernadette, Madame Psychosis, Bombardier, and Luddie—meet and understand one another immediately.

Dear Luddie,

When I say "we" I mean Bernadette and me.

When I say "we" I mean Madame Psychosis, and his lover, Bernadette.

Madame Psychosis loves Bernadette and Bernadette loves Madame Psychosis.

Bernadette doesn't know the laws of the Midwest, or the Bombardier, but because she loves me she's coming to Poland to find you, and because I love her she's coming to Poland to find you, but despite our love for one another we are roped down in Chicago without the Bombardier, far away from you.

But it isn't as hopeless as it sounds because we, at least, are together, though we miss the Bombardier. The woman in the blue suit has told us the Bombardier will be here as soon as we finish our chewy nachos at the airport bar, so we wait.

We wait because Bernadette believes what we've been told, and I'm afraid I believe it too, despite what I know to be true about the Midwest and its roots and laws. I know about its roots and laws because, like the Bombardier, I was born in the Midwest, but unlike the Bombardier I had hoped to fly away from the Midwest for good when I turned eighteen. I had hoped to never come back.

Dear Luddie,

She is beautiful too.

Bernadette, I mean.

She is beautiful and that she is beautiful helps me understand what I mean when I say "we." That she is beautiful should help you to understand what I mean when I say "we," but I have learned some people are immune to beautiful things. I have learned that my brother who once turned green with nausea beside me as I cut open a fish is now immune. He could cut open one hundred fish now when I couldn't cut open one. He could cut open one hundred fish because beautiful things cannot affect him. Beautiful things cannot affect him because he has been brained by power and uniforms.

He is a Marine, Luddie.

The few, the proud, my brother, Luddie.

I have not been brained by power or uniforms, not a Marine, and so I cannot cut open a fish. Beautiful things have affected me so many times I am crippled by a pathetic gentleness, and this crippling keeps me from cutting open any fish, from killing anything.

Bernadette is beautiful and her beauty has crippled me to the point of nearly full abstraction. When I think of her beauty I don't think of sidewalks or cars or flowers or candy, I think of yellow and orange and democracy. I think of yellow and orange and democracy, but, it's true, I also think of her face as she goes about her day. I think of her beauty, and I think of her face as she sells a birdfeeder. She is beautiful, and she sells a birdfeeder to a man in New England.

I think of her soft, brown-eyed, perfect-nosed face as these people come into the store where she works selling birdfeeders. I think of her slightly sideways smile as these people tell her crazy things about beautiful birds. They tell her crazy things about beautiful birds and ugly squirrels and wandering bears and strange moose, and she smiles her slightly sideways smile as they tell her.

One man, who often told her crazy things about beautiful birds, once brought in a photograph of a strange moose. This photograph of a strange moose made her smile slightly even more sideways.

In this photograph, this strange moose stands ghostly and antler-less against a black background of budding trees. It stares into the camera as if the camera were a part of this black background of budding trees but a part of the black background of budding trees that is also full of wolves.

It is an albino moose and it is beautiful.

Bernadette loves the albino moose because she doesn't believe the black background could be full of anything like wolves, only other beautiful things like the albino moose.

It could be full of other albino moose, but it also could be full of yellow-bellied sapsuckers. This is not hard to believe, because yellow-bellied sapsuckers can be seen if you know where to look. If you know, you look at the edge of the black forest of budding trees.

It is not hard to believe in the yellow-bellied sapsucker, but the yellow-bellied sapsucker is not often talked about in the birdfeeding store, because it is not a real bird-feeder bird or an albino and so is not rare or common. It is simply beautiful and believable.

The beautiful and believable yellow-bellied sapsucker can be seen just on the edge of the black forest full of wolves, or the edge of what the albino moose looks at, depending on what you believe.

I believe Bernadette, who is more beautiful than the albino moose or the yellow-bellied sapsucker, who has brown eyes and a little ice cream belly. She has an old cotton T-shirt and wiggling toes. She has a low laugh and warm hands.

I believe her and I live with her in New England.

In New England, we live in a rented row house with two friends we call Big B and Medium B, along with our two cats, Little B and Pree.

We drink wine together and tell stories about where we grew up and the books we loved—*Ramona Quimby, Age 8, Tales of a Fourth Grade Nothing, A Wrinkle in Time, Bruno and Boots*. We collect records, dishes, tablecloths, and books.

We are romantic and adventurous, and we tell everyone about our romances and our adventures in poems, songs, and stories.

Bernadette and I are romantic and adventurous and friends and together we're going on an adventure to find a lost love, Luddie, and when we get back we'll tell our friends all about it. We'll drink wine. We'll tell stories. That's why we're here.

Bernadette and I.

We're lovers, but we have had no babies.

We tell stories.

This is what I mean when I say "we."

Dear Luddie,

Let me tell you something else.

Let me tell you that every once in a while, I spot a spindly red hair in the boring brown sideburns that grow like moss on my face.

Is that interesting?

I'm trying to make an interesting story while we wait for the Bombardier to arrive in his little plane from Des Moines, so let me tell you something else.

Let me tell you that one summer I let the moss grow into a beard. This beard covered most of my long, horsy face. On my long cheeks and my horsy chin, a few red patches grew in the normal brown clumps.

Let me tell you that I pulled at these red patches. I patted them when I sat in my chair at the bookstore where I work, daydreaming about the strange names in the Bombardier's family.

Let me tell you that there have been some strange names in the Bombardier's family: Lorn, Zebulon, Cave, and Beulah.

Duey, Maurice, Virgil, and Soledad.

Let me tell you that every once in a while, like my drunk, dead, red-headed great-grandfather, who was named not Anthony but Toni, I want to ride with a wild red beard flying behind me on a railroad car away from everything I know.

I want to make that kind of interesting story.

It is possible to make that kind of interesting story in America, Luddie, even now, but I've never done it because my beard was not full and red but patchy, boring, and brown.

I am trying to be a good man.

I am trying to be a good man, so I've never made that kind of interesting story. I've tried to make a story about going to Germany and to Poland with the Bombardier and Bernadette, but so far it isn't interesting at all.

I'm stuck with my plain brown hair, plain mossy sideburns, plain name, and no beard here in Chicago with Bernadette. We're four hours late, and I don't think we will ever leave.

Dear Luddie,

That was not interesting.

I'm sorry.

That was not a story.

The airport light has maybe gotten into my brain and so my stories aren't interesting.

A story must be interesting, so let me tell you that Bernadette and I are still in Chicago, still held down by brown and black roots and weird laws even though we've finished our chewy nachos at the airport bar.

Is that interesting?

Okay, let me tell you something else.

Let me tell you something interesting while we wait.

Let me tell you a story.

Let me tell you a story where something interesting happens but first let me tell you something about interesting things. Interesting things don't happen quickly.

Nothing happens quickly, but only horribly and strangely slow.

Dear Luddie,

Let me tell you something about the horrible strangeness of what happens in Chicago.

What happens is Bernadette and I stay in Chicago, in the Midwest, longer than a minute. We stay in Chicago longer than a minute because we have nowhere else to go.

What happens is the Bombardier stays in the sky, slowly leaving by weird laws of physics from Des Moines.

What happens here in Chicago is that Bernadette and I eat at the airport bar.

We eat some chewy nachos at the airport bar and a man in a tan hat sitting across from us sends his steak back to be re-cooked three times.

After we eat our chewy nachos and after the Bombardier doesn't arrive in Chicago, we wait. We watch this man eat his bloody greasy steak with a plastic fork, and I think of another story. After we watch the man eat his bloody greasy steak, and I think of another story, I tell this story to Bernadette because we are together, and people when they are together tell stories to each other, right?

Right.

These stories must have characters, plots, and settings.

These stories must do things with time.

They must be interesting.

Think of this man eating his bloody greasy steak, and you will see what I mean.

A man in a tan hat.

Sending the steak back.

In Chicago.

Over and over and over again.

Character, plot, setting, time.

The story I tell to Bernadette after we watch "The Man in the Tan Hat and His Bloody Greasy Steak" has characters, a plot, and a setting.

It has time.

Bernadette and I settle into our seats.

I begin a story to pass the time.

"He was the lead Bombardier in a squadron of planes bombing an oil factory in Poland," I begin, "the oil factory called Blechhammer."

In my mind, I see my words flowing from this silvery fountain pen onto a sepia page as I speak them. It's a classic story. A TV story.

"The Air Force allowed men to go home after fifty missions," I say, "and the Bombardier had flown forty-nine missions. He had flown forty-nine missions, and he had learned to site the target in his scope and to let the bombs fall through the sky onto the target. He had learned to listen on the radio for 'I'll Be Seeing You' before every mission, because, so far, he had heard Bing Crosby sing 'I'll be seeing you in all the old familiar places,' and he had lived through every mission.

"This mission was to be his last mission before going home to see everyone in all the old familiar places," I say, "and everyone in the plane dreaded it, because they knew the Germans guarded Blechhammer with as much flack and anti-aircraft artillery as almost anywhere else in their domain."

Bernadette scratches her little ice cream belly through her old cotton T-shirt. She rests her chin on her warm hand.

She listens.

"They flew free and clear from their base in Foggia, Italy to Blechhammer," I say, "but once they got within a few hundred miles of the Blechhammer, they began to see the guns of the German fighters flashing in the sky around them.

"This was December 26, 1944.

"By the time they got to the initial point, where the Bombardier was to take over for the pilot and guide the plane to the target, all of their guns were hot, and they had been hit by German fire. The flack had been heavy too, so their plane began sputtering, smoking, and wheezing.

"The Bombardier sat in the nose of the sputtering, smoking, wheezing plane. He sat in the nose and so he was the first thing over the target, the lead squadron, and so everyone on our side was relying on him to see through the smoke and the clouds to Blechhammer to drop those bombs.

"And despite their sputtering, smoking, and wheezing, they held on.

"As soon as the Bombardier saw those thimble-sized vats in the scope, he let his bombs loose.

"He couldn't see through the smoke or the clouds to see what they hit, but he let his bombs loose through the air."

I make a motion in the air with my hand like throwing water onto a hot frying pan.

"After that," I go on, "they rattled along as best they could. The co-pilot's leg had been blown off, the radar man had gone into shock, and their engines had gone out, but despite it all they crash-landed into a field in Rzeszów, Poland.

"Everyone in the plane seemed okay, except the co-pilot, whose leg had been blown off by the flack and whose face looked whiter than bone.

"Flack, you see, is a kind of anti-aircraft artillery."

Bernadette nods. She knows about flack, but she knows that explaining flack is part of the story. Because explaining flack is part of the story, she nods.

She smiles.

She likes waiting with this storyteller. I can feel it. Waiting isn't so bad.

"They crashed into a field and they saw men running through the field toward them. Weeks before, the Bombardier's best friend had crashed

32

into a field in Czechoslovakia. The Bombardier's best friend had crashed terribly, but he had lived through the impact. Then men with pitchforks had come running through the field. They killed him. They jabbed pitchforks into the Bombardier's best friend until he was dead.

"The Bombardier, now crashed in a field, watched men running toward his plane, and he thought of his friend jabbed by pitchforks, and so he reached for his revolver, but then he saw that the men running toward his plane did not have pitchforks. The men running toward his plane did not have guns. They had moustaches," I say, as the waitress takes the chewy nacho plate away, "they were Poles, and they had moustaches, and they did not kill the Bombardier with pitchforks."

"What a story!" Bernadette says, rubbing her feet together under the table.

"Oh yes," I say, "It is very dramatic."

Dear Luddie,

Was it really very dramatic in 1944?

Had you heard many stories like this one in your little town by 1944?

Did the Bombardier tell you this dramatic story the first night, after you saw him fall from the sky in the flaming B-17, exhausted, with cuts and bruises from the crash?

Did you like his voice?

He has a clear voice, like a silver light emanating from a fountain pen.

Did you lean over a wooden table with a bowl of soup as he told you his story?

Did he smell like green aftershave?

Or did he tell you his story later, in small pieces, reluctantly, as he helped peel potatoes for dinner, or as he chopped firewood, cleaning the snow from a stump with his hands?

Dear Luddie,

The Bombardier told me his story in small blocks.

He told me his story in small blocks as I grew up.

I felt my puny story grow in the shadow of his story, but there have always been blocks missing from his story.

I've never felt like I understood his story completely, and yet it has always stood tall.

Now, in the airport, I try to tell Bernadette his story in small blocks from the ground up.

I place each detailed block carefully and precisely in front of her, but I do not place the blocks slowly.

Bernadette has a few hours for this story, but she doesn't have years to grow up in its shadow, so the blocks pile up very fast in the airport.

The blocks pile up very fast, like a long train speeding into the sky, and some blocks remain obscure to me even though the story is the oldest one I know.

I wonder, for example, about the men with moustaches.

Were they the Polish Underground, or were they Russian soldiers, or were they just men living through the war near a field?

The Polish Underground would be a green block, a Russian soldier would be a red block, and a man living through the war would be a yellow block.

I know the color of the block is a small thing to not know, but even the smallest block supports other, bigger blocks, more important blocks, so I have to know even the small unknown things to get the story right, so I'm worried.

I'm worried that if I focus too closely on the small green, red, or yellow blocks, I won't be able to see the patterns of the Bombardier's story. If I am not able to see the patterns as the blocks rush past me into the sky, then my version of his story will become like a home movie that focuses in on the street as the building above it bursts into flames.

"Did you see that?" the spectators will shout, "What happened?"

"I don't know, I don't know," I'll say, my breathy voice and clicking hands rubbing on the microphone. "I was looking at the street, that dog . . ."

In other words, my version of his story will be confused.

I don't want my version of his story to be confused, so I ask myself, would I be a better correspondent if I blurred my eyes and waited for the patterns to crowd my vision, or would I be a better correspondent if I inspected every small block as if I had all the time in the world?

I don't know the answer, but I ask myself about these blocks and patterns all the time.

When I'm trying to sleep, when I'm walking to the post office, when I'm sitting on a plane, I ask myself.

I ask myself all the time, but when I ask myself about the blocks this time, I misplace some more blocks as I build this towering story.

"They went with the men with moustaches to a barn and stayed the night," I say to Bernadette, "and the next day they walked further to a little town where two Russian soldiers took them in."

Panya and Maya are two strange blocks.

"Panya and Maya," I say, "marched them to Luddie's home, which really was just a little cottage with a straw roof. They all stayed the night huddled on her dirt floor, and then in the morning Luddie led them all to the dugout where they would be safe from the Nazis."

I wonder if I need to know why they called the Russians Panya and Maya? Do I need to know more about the Panya and Maya blocks for his towering story to be clear?

I don't know.

I do know, though, that I need to know about your little cottage.

I need to know about your little cottage for our story to make sense.

Our story, Luddie.

Our big, important story.

Our clear story.

Our not-confused story.

I know that you and your family were in the Polish Underground and that you took the Bombardier in and sheltered him from the enemy in your little cottage.

Your little cottage on your street in Rzeszów.

I know someone has written the name of your street on the back of your photograph.

I know that you were the translator and protector for these men in December of 1944.

"The Bombardier and his crew stayed in the dugout with Panya and Maya," I say, "from December 26, 1944 into the middle of January 1945.

"They grew very restless in that month, because the dugout was just a narrow hole in the ground with woodburning stoves on either end. No man slept without his pistol in his hand, because no one knew who might discover them.

"The Bombardier has said to me, 'Thank God Luddie was there to translate some of Panya and Maya's babble, or there would have surely been bloodshed.'

"There was no bloodshed.

"Panya was a big dumb Russian with what they called a push broom moustache," I say, making it up, "and he was always wanting to wrestle."

"The Bombardier has told me," I say to Bernadette, "'Of all things in that little dugout, this oaf wanted to wrestle!'"

"Did he?" Bernadette asks.

She's excited.

"Did he what?" I ask.

"Wrestle!"

"Good God! No," I say, "Panya was huge!"

I picture the Bombardier rubbing his hands together and laughing at the memory of Panya and Maya. I rub my hands together a little.

"No," I say, "He steered clear of both of them as best he could, because Panya wanted to wrestle and Maya liked to clean his gun. They were a very showy couple, those two, but the Bombardier and his men stayed with this showy couple until the American planes came and transported them back to a base in Russia, where they stayed until February 1945.

"Eventually," I say, "they transferred to Tehran, Iran, then Cairo, Egypt, and finally back to Foggia, Italy, where they began."

"That's quite a trip," Bernadette says.

She looks at me, smiling at the trip, but I am wringing my hands now, not smiling.

"Oh yes. I think he would have enjoyed it too," I say, "had they not been declared missing."

As I say this, I see the Bombardier leaning back in his chair and touching his bottom lip with his finger.

And then I can't picture him at all.

For a moment, he goes missing.

As he goes missing, I feel a block go tumbling through the trees.

I stop wringing my hands and try to chase this tumbling block with my mind.

"Picture him!" I whisper to Bernadette, "Picture him sitting in the back of an Army jeep! His sleeves are rolled up high! He's waiting in the sweltering heat of Iran!"

Bernadette plays along, leaning over to me and whispering back, "He's laughing a little, but his face is obscure."

His face is obscure. We lose him.

We can't catch this barreling block with our minds as it falls into oblivion.

It is sixty years after his story, and we can't picture his face in Iran, or Egypt, or Russia, or Poland, and this worries me.

Can you picture his face in Poland, Luddie? Have I made it any clearer?

Dear Luddie,

As we sit in the gate area, waiting for the Bombardier, I close my eyes and try not to think about the tumbling blocks of history.

What's the point?

I try to conjure the Bombardier's face in my mind instead of the tumbling blocks of history.

I close my eyes and try to bring the Bombardier into our waiting world in Chicago, but all I see are blocks tumbling through the trees into oblivion.

I see Panya and Maya, guns and vodka, tree stumps and falling planes and moustaches.

I see the Bombardier, Luddie, but vaguely.

An interesting story must have characters, Luddie, but the characters in the interesting story should not tumble through the trees.

If the characters tumble through the trees then the story is not a story but a worried mash of blurry sketches with no beginning and no end tumbling through the trees forever.

I want to tell the Bombardier's story, but all I see are leaves bending and branches breaking.

I'm confused.

I wonder, when you close your eyes, Luddie, can you conjure the face of the Bombardier?

Do dead faces and breaking branches interfere?

Sometimes, when dead faces and breaking branches don't interfere, I can conjure the Bombardier as a pure character in a great story.

I close my eyes, and instead of a floating dead face, I see a sidewalk and a small brick house. I see a man in front of it and I see that this man in front of the small brick house is short and stocky. I see that he has the face of a tall, regal man. His thin hair in a recessed part. Its fine silver thread in an arc.

He is the Bombardier. He is the mayor of his small town in the Midwest.

I see his high forehead, his thin silver hair, his long, downturned nose. His droopy eyelids.

I see his wide brisket covered by a sweater, and then there are his stocky legs.

I see that he is short, but he is smiling and pleasant, in a red flannel shirt and sky blue Wrangler jeans. A cellophane bag of peanuts rests in his shirt pocket, half eaten with the top right corner of the bag torn open, but no peanuts spill because the Bombardier has folded the bag neatly in half.

The peanuts are safe for later.

He stands squarely like a solid character in a real story. He has good posture, but walking out of the airplane, as I hoped he would do shortly, I expected to see him leaning forward a bit, as he does when he is determined to get somewhere.

In my mind, I want him to wave at me, but I don't see him clearly enough.

When I try too hard to see him clearly I only see a dead, blue, bulging face with Venus flytrap eyes, hanging from a tree.

Dear Luddie,

When I open my eyes I don't see faces or trees, only a little plane on the tarmac.

A little plane on the tarmac, the Bombardier's little plane from Des Moines.

I feel a new story beginning.

My hand begins to sweat and I stand up, but then I get confused, so I sit back down. My heart races, and I give Bernadette a one-armed shoulder hug. She hunches her shoulders into my arm and smiles.

"Here he is!" she says.

Here he is, I think, and look at the dark doorway of the little plane, but I don't see him.

I see another character from another story is in the way of our new story.

There is another character in the way of the Bombardier, and this other character is a stock character.

This stock character stands in the doorway of the plane. A big, clownish man in a sweatshirt stands in the doorway of the little plane chatting with the stewardess. A big piece of pink meat in a sweatshirt stands in front of our story.

I feel our story dissolving into his story.

Right then, I hate this man's story more than I've hated anything in my life.

I've heard this man's story over and over again.

I've heard it over and over again and it's about college football and beer and real estate and I feel despair creeping over me, because I don't want to be any part of this story anymore.

Everyone knows this story and everyone knows it has no adventure and no romance. It's bad history, Luddie, no one needs it. I tell myself this in anger, but secretly I know that even this story can be heroic in its way. One of those memories forcing the current one way or the other.

But now, waiting for the Bombardier, the panic rises in my throat like blood, and I think our story truly might dissolve completely into this boring meat man's story, this man who is not a hero. Then, something new and interesting happens.

Something new and interesting happens in our story, and it is that the Bombardier appears from the darkness of the little plane from Des Moines.

3

Dear Luddie,

When the Bombardier emerges from the darkness of the little plane, I don't have to try to conjure him anymore.

I see him.

The romantic hero of our adventure.

Here he is.

I see him and he is dressed in a brown tweed suit, brown tie, leather boots, and a jaunty, dark brown hat with a small feather in it.

As he walks out to us, I see his tie has a perfect teardrop in the center of the knot.

When I was a boy, I remember this hero telling me, "The ladies go for a man with the teardrop in the center of the knot." Every time he wore a tie, the teardrop sat in the center of the knot.

The ladies went for him.

In my life, when I wear a tie, the teardrop never sits in the center of the knot but always off to the side, like it's painfully squirting out of some strange hole in the side of the tie.

It's embarrassing when I wear a tie, Luddie.

With his perfectly teardropped tie, the Bombardier strides out to us, leaning forward slightly. My hands feel wooly. I push my hair out of my eyes with my wooly hands.

He is unharmed.

We rush over to meet him.

"I sure am glad to see you two!" he says.

I reach out to touch him.

Dear Luddie,

I don't know if you remember, but the Bombardier's voice is always clear and strong. It is clear and strong but it is not overbearing or bullying.

In my mind, I always hear him saying in his clear and strong voice the word, "Chicago" like a silver light emanating from a fountain pen. The word has two long "o" sounds in his mouth, like "pogo."

"Here we are in Chicago," he says in Chicago, gently pushing my enthusiastic hug away and reaching for Bernadette.

They hug.

"It sure is nice to meet you," he says, adjusting his tie.

Bernadette beams.

Already, I think she's going for him!

Dear Luddie,

The plan is that all together, we will wait in Chicago, and then all together we will fly to Frankfurt, Germany.

We will all fly to Frankfurt, Germany together, and then to Berlin, and then finally we will drive on to Poland where we will find you.

That will be a story with a point, and I will tell it to you when it happens, but for now our plan is just to wait.

That is the plan.

Waiting.

We wait and waiting is a good time for stories, so, as we sit looking out at the sun setting on the tarmac, Bernadette asks the Bombardier about his stories.

The Bombardier, with his silver-light voice, can tell a great story.

He puts his boot up on a rail in the airport and asks with a small smile, "Do you really want to hear a story?"

Bernadette laughs.

"I'm here, aren't I?" she says.

"There was a time," the Bombardier says, patting her on the cheek, "when I would never tell this kind of story to anyone, not even my wife. But now, it seems, no one can stop me from telling stories. No one can shut me up!"

"It's okay," Bernadette says, "I don't want to shut you up."

Her sideways smile smiles.

"Well," the Bombardier says with a shrug, "This story begins in 1966."

I clear my throat and rub my sweaty hands on my pants, sink in my seat a little and squirm.

I know this story.

This is not a story I want to hear.

This story has characters, it's true. This story has the Bombardier and a man named Willie, the Bombardier's radical daughter, and the police.

49

This story has sex, death, the Midwest, Chicago, and time.

This is a good story, I think, but it's confusing.

It's not a story I would tell, but the Bombardier is not me, and so he begins.

"When I returned to the Midwest after the war," he says to Bernadette, "I married a girl from Chicago.

"This girl from Chicago and I had a happy life together, and we had a daughter."

Bernadette nods and reaches over our armrest to squeeze my hand. I squeeze back and try to smile at her but the smile is weak.

"By the time my daughter turned eighteen," the Bombardier goes on, "I had willy-nilly become the mayor of this little Midwest town, and my daughter, well, she had become a radical."

He looks down at his tie and gives it a little shake.

"A radical," he says again.

"What about before she turned eighteen?" Bernadette asks.

"Before she turned eighteen?" the Bombardier echoes, looking up.

"Before she turned eighteen," he says, "the radical daughter had been a string bean girl, a girl with books held to her chest and her head pointed down, a reader with worlds inside her head but no words to describe them.

"Boring," the Bombardier says with a smile, "but she was my little girl."

"Boring?" Bernadette asks.

"Truthfully, she really was boring," the Bombardier says with a small nod of his head, "But when she turned eighteen all of that hidden, inner richness burst out."

"Are you going to say she blossomed?" Bernadette asks, squinting her eyes and cocking her head to the side.

"Yes," the Bombardier laughs, "I am going to say she blossomed. She bloomed! She burst at the seams when she turned eighteen! I couldn't believe it! My little girl!

"She grew and she stretched and where she grew she got stretch marks, but the men did not notice the stretch marks, they only noticed where she grew."

"That's what they do," Bernadette says with a sigh and rolls her eyes at me.

The Bombardier laughs.

I do not.

"Well," he says, "she did. She bloomed. She blossomed. And she got a boyfriend. A boyfriend who was black."

Bernadette's hand squeezes mine a little tighter. I feel her hand squeeze mine a little tighter and so I try to let my hand go slack. There's nothing to worry about, I try to say with my hand, but there is.

"Yes," the Bombardier says, "My radical daughter, once she turned eighteen, not only blossomed, burst, and bloomed, but pushed this blossoming bursting bloom against a black man. Something that was not done in our town! No way!"

He looks down again at his tie and becomes quiet.

"The town where you were the mayor?" Bernadette asks.

"That's right," the Bombardier says, "where I was the mayor. My town, the mayor's town, a town famous for its whiteness."

I can feel the grains in my sweat grinding into Bernadette's palm.

"Its what?" she asks.

"Its whiteness," the Bombardier says, clearing his throat, "now, please, no more interruptions."

Bernadette blinks once and makes a gesture with her hand. The hand that had held mine.

"Go on," the gesture could be saying.

Or "Stop."

The Bombardier goes on.

"Newspapers, magazines, and TV shows," he says, "made my town famous for its whiteness. They called it 'The Whitest Town in America' and descended upon it with all of their weapons—their microphones, their steno pads, and their cameras.

"They reported into their weapons that my town's 'sameness, its effortless conservation against a tide of change in America, is truly remarkable.'

"They made my town famous, a symbol of something I'm sure, though I'll be damned if I know what.

"'This is just how we've turned out,' I said to the radio, the magazines, and the TV. 'We didn't plan to be so white. Is it wrong?'

"'When the Watts riots burned,' the radio, the magazines, and the TV said, 'the Whitest Town in America shrugged. When they threw rocks at Martin Luther King, Jr. in Chicago, the Whitest Town in America rolled its eyes, and when Brown went up against the Board of Education, the Whitest Town in America went about its business.

"'Because,' the radio, the magazines, and the TV went on, 'its business wasn't black. Its business was farming and insurance and Avon. Its business was white, white, white!'"

Small flecks of spittle have formed on the Bombardier's thin lips.

He licks them away after he says white, white, white.

"I just shrugged," he says, "Why all this fuss? My town had its business, sure, and it was all those things—farming, insurance, Avon. It was white. So what?"

"When does this story take place?" Bernadette asks.

The sunlight has begun to fade. Everything is orange.

"This story takes place in 1966," the Bombardier says in the orange.

"Got it," Bernadette says in the orange and sips from a bottle of water.

Dear Luddie,

Over the loudspeaker, I hear a voice call our flight number. I hear it in the orange as Bernadette drinks from her water bottle with a hand that doesn't hold mine. Our flight to Frankfurt.

"What?" Bernadette says.

"The End," I say, putting my things back into my backpack, "that's it. We should get to the gate."

The Bombardier, lost in thought for a moment, blinks once and agrees.

"Yes, let's get to the gate," he says.

"What happened in 1966?" Bernadette whispers to me as we walk toward the gate.

"It's just some pointless story," I say.

"What do you mean?" she says.

"I mean it's a weird story and it's pointless and it was the sixties," I say. "All kinds of crazy things happened."

"What happened to his daughter?"

"Nothing, I guess. She got married later, had kids."

"Nothing?" Bernadette says.

"Nothing," I say, "That's the story!"

"That," Bernadette says as we walk from the vinyl chairs to the gate, "is not a story. What's the point?"

I think for a moment about the point.

"I have barely even met this Bombardier and he's telling me this crazy story about his 'radical' daughter," she says.

"It doesn't have a point, I guess," I say. "Not every story has a point. Sometimes you just tell them. And she was radical. Your family doesn't have stories like this?"

"No," Bernadette says with a hard look.

We don't talk about her family much.

"Stories have points," she says "That story has a point, you just don't know it."

"What do you think the point is, then?" I ask.

"The point?" she says, "The point is that you and the Bombardier have messed up ideas about what's boring and what's pointless. That's the point."

Dear Luddie,

If I make it clear enough it won't matter what the point is.

It won't matter what I think is boring or pointless.

It won't matter when the Bombardier goes missing.

It won't matter when he goes missing because I will have made him clear and real as a character in a story, and a clear and real character can be a correspondent. A clear and real character in a story can be a correspondent between the living and the dead. A clear and real correspondent in a story joins the hands of ghosts with the hands of the living, but I have neither been nor created a clear and real correspondent, yet.

Let me try to be clear then, Luddie.

Let me try to be clear about what really happens.

Dear Luddie,

What really happens is that we go to the gate to get on our flight to Frankfurt. We go together after listening to the Bombardier's story.

Wait.

Let me try to be clear about who we are.

We are Madame Psychosis, Bernadette, and the Bombardier.

Madame Psychosis is twenty-four-year-old me.

Bernadette is beautiful and calm Bernadette with wide brown eyes.

The Bombardier is eighty-four-year-old the Bombardier, a Rotarian with a story, a former mayor.

Let me be clear about his story.

His story begins in December 1944, but it continues for sixty years into December of 2004.

In December of 2004, the Bombardier told me that more than anything he wanted to return to Poland before he died. More than anything he wanted to return to where he had been shot down by the Nazis in December 1944.

In December 1944, the Bombardier hid in Rzeszów.

He hid in the dugout with Panya and Maya and he hid in the house with you, Luddie, and he hid in the grass from the last of the Nazis.

Let me be clear about the Bombardier crouched in the weeds along the gravel road at night in Rzeszów.

His jacket is green.

He holds his breath as a black car passes against the wheat.

The last of the Nazis.

Let me be clear that sixty years later, the Bombardier is flying back to Poland where he dropped hundreds of bombs on hundreds of targets during World War II.

Sixty years later, he is returning without bombs but with a story to tell.

He wanted to return alone. The lone Bombardier returning, but then he burned a kitchen towel on the stove. A Christmas dinner. The kitchen towel burned, and he didn't notice until his radical daughter saw the flames from the dining room table.

"Dad!" she yelled. "You're going to burn us all to death!"

As the Bombardier watched his radical daughter smother the burning towel, he asked his radical daughter if she would go with him to Poland to see where he dropped his bombs. His radical daughter stopped smothering the towel and sighed.

Her brown hair was short now, dyed blond, spiky.

"I can't do it, Dad," she said and sighed again.

She was too busy with her life in America to go to Poland with the Bombardier.

I saw the towel burn and I saw his radical daughter smother it. I heard him ask his radical daughter, and I heard her sigh.

I knew I was not like his radical daughter. I knew I would not be so busy with my life in America.

I knew Bernadette and I could try to be a witness and a doorknob.

We could try.

We are trying.

We will try, but we will have to try harder because, you'll see, we've already lost him.

Dear Luddie,

Am I being clear?

Do you understand?

If we take the Bombardier to Germany and Poland, I will be his doorknob and Bernadette will be our witness, and no towels will burn. No
one will see flames from the dining room table.

Right?

No.

I'm not being clear.

Let me start again.

Dear Luddie,

Where was I?

Oh yes.

I remember.

I was going to Germany and then to Poland with Bernadette and the Bombardier.

The day before I left with Bernadette to meet the Bombardier, I read in the newspaper that the tracks to Atocha station in Spain had been blown up by terrorists.

A train had been on the tracks.

Two hundred people had died.

"All travelers are soldiers now," a man in a beret at the bookstore had told my boss.

"What are we fighting for?" my boss asked.

The man in the beret shrugged.

I watched them closely because Bernadette and I would soon be travelers and perhaps soldiers in Chicago with the Bombardier, but my boss and this man in the beret had no answers.

When Bernadette and I arrived in Chicago, we rushed off the plane to make our connection to Frankfurt with the Bombardier, but we couldn't find the Bombardier anywhere in the crowded blue gate area.

You know this story.

We rushed onto the plane that was to take us with the Bombardier to Frankfurt but we couldn't find him on the plane either.

Maybe, we thought, he had been blown up like Atocha station.

Like good soldiers though, we stopped thinking about being blown up and we listened to a faceless automaton in a blue suit.

The faceless automaton in a blue suit said the Bombardier's flight from Des Moines had been delayed four hours.

Like good soldiers, the other travelers listened to the faceless automaton in a suit.

A few yelled and were rude.

One man barked, "Are you fucking serious?"

This barking man was not a good soldier.

Hours later, after the Bombardier's plane showed up, we listened to the Bombardier almost tell a story of 1966 with his boot on the rail.

Remember?

I told you this before in a story we may now call, "Almost Building a Tower of History in Chicago."

After the story, "Almost Building a Tower of History in Chicago," we are all caught up.

Dear Luddie,

We are all caught up and here we are waiting to board the flight to Germany.

Trying to board the nine o'clock flight, all caught up, we run into a new faceless automaton in a blue suit.

This faceless automaton in a blue suit has never heard of "Building a Tower of History in Chicago."

When we tell her about it, she shrugs and tells us to wait with the other travelers for the overbooked nine o'clock flight.

Like a good soldier, the Bombardier politely tells the faceless automaton that he understands why she can't help "Building a Tower of History in Chicago" turn into "The Flight to Frankfurt."

He tells her that mistakes happen in stories, that some stories are better than others.

She tells us someone will call our names, so, like good soldiers, we sit down to wait for our names to be called.

I remember when I was in high school I fantasized about punching myself in the face.

In the fantasy, I am sitting on my chest with my mouth clenched, thrusting my fist into my face until there is nothing left of my face.

This is the only kind of soldier I have ever wanted to be, Luddie.

Near the counter, other travelers are yelling and carrying on, being rude to the faceless automatons.

One traveler says, "This is some ridiculous shit," and his face comes into stark relief against the rigid pattern on the wall.

The Bombardier watches this traveler and then sits down to tell us another story.

"During the war," he says, patting the seat beside him, inviting Bernadette to sit, "I knew a soldier who had the filthiest mouth."

Bernadette sits down beside him and listens to his story.

"Every other word out of this soldier's mouth was a curse word or an epithet," the Bombardier says, gesturing to the filthy-mouthed man, "I thought it was disgusting. I thought, 'Only someone with a very poor vocabulary would have to use so many curse words and epithets.'

"But, it turned out that this soldier had a pretty good vocabulary," the Bombardier chuckles. "His name was Joseph Heller, and he went on to write a book about the war called *Catch-22*. I've heard many people enjoy it, but I'm sure it's filled with curse words and epithets, so I've never read it."

Bernadette and I laugh at this story called "Joseph Heller's Filthy Mouth."

There are thousands of questions to ask about this story but the airport has made us dumb, so we just laugh.

After we laugh our dumb laughs, we look around us.

Around us, each of the yelling, rude travelers are boarding, including the well-defined, filthy-mouthed man.

No one calls our names.

After a few more assurances from the faceless automatons that we will all make it on the flight, it becomes clearer and clearer we will not.

Even though it has become clearer and clearer we will not all make it on the flight, we politely defer and accept the faceless automaton's apologies like good soldiers in a catch-22.

Some previous faceless automaton, the faceless automaton tells us, hadn't properly put us "in the system" so now this new faceless automaton is powerless to help us.

She says there is no "comment" by our names, and then she shakes her faceless automaton head.

Her faceless automaton head is a pale tan color, smooth and curved, with auburn hair framing its strange egg.

At the last second, the strange egg automaton bleats my name through a speaker and offers me one seat.

"One seat?" I say to the strange egg automaton, "I can't take one seat."

"I can't go to Frankfurt with the Bombardier in one seat," I say, "in one seat I can't take Bernadette, whose skin is soft and tan like the surface of Saturn."

I say this, but the faceless automaton says "One seat"—her lips, tongue, and teeth emerge from the smooth, egg surface and spit, "Take it or leave it," then flatten back into a placid, smooth thing.

A long string of curse words and epithets begins to uncoil within me, but before this string can burst out onto this faceless automaton, the Bombardier takes his hotel information and a few Euros from my backpack. He touches my arm.

"I'll take the one seat," he says.

He says he will take the one seat and we will meet him at his hotel in Berlin.

I swallow the string of curse words and epithets, and I stammer something about eighty-four and no German and *Catch-22*, but the Bombardier salutes Bernadette and boards the plane without us.

The flight closes and the plane takes off into the sky with the Bombardier.

Bernadette and I stand on the ground with the faceless automatons. The faceless automatons again apologize and chastise the blundering faceless automatons that came before them.

"You will be on the next flight out," she bleats, "we'll confirm you in the morning."

"Did you put a comment by our names?" Bernadette asks.

"Oh yes," she says, "I put a comment by your names. Don't worry about that."

We wander out into the sea of other travelers, uncomplaining and silent, like good soldiers.

Dear Luddie,

When I was a boy I used to wonder if I could be a "Wolverine."

Could I be a "Wolverine," like in the movie *Red Dawn,* pissing in the radiator and shooting at the Russians from behind winter trees?

Would I survive without American order?

When I rode my bike down steep hills I got scared. When I rode my bike down steep hills I got scared, so I had my doubts if I could be a "Wolverine."

American order kept me from having to ride my bike down steep hills if I didn't want to.

After a night of a little sleep and a lot of steep hill dreams in the faceless automaton hotel in Chicago, Bernadette and I get to the airport three hours early.

An earthy clamp calls me as yellow ropes pull me from the sky in my dream. It's a dream of blue sky falling all around me and too soon the earth.

When we get to the check-in counter three hours early, the new faceless automaton tells us last night's faceless automaton did not do a proper job, and so this new faceless automaton doesn't know anything about "Building a Tower of History in Chicago" or "The Bombardier Leaves Us in Chicago" or "Riding My Bike Down Steep Hills in a Time of War" or "The Dream of Earthy Clamps."

She doesn't have any seats for us.

We very politely and calmly try to tell our stories to this new faceless automaton. We tell her our stories as if our stories aren't becoming ridiculous and tiresome, pointless stories.

"We have an eighty-four-year-old man in a foreign country we need to be with," we say.

"We have already waited through two flights. We have already lost a day of our trip," we say.

64

"We are good soldiers," we say.

The faceless automaton nods. She says good soldiers sign up for the Preferred Customer program. Signing up for the Preferred Customer program, she says, will make us really good soldiers.

"Could we tell our stories to your supervisor?" we ask.

After ten bleary minutes, the supervisor of this faceless automaton walks through the blur of other travelers. He walks fast and speaks gruffly into a walkie-talkie.

Speaking gruffly into a walkie-talkie, the supervisor of the faceless automaton has a peachy mass on his neck that every once in a while congeals into something resembling a face.

I want to punch it.

The peachy-mass-faced supervisor of this faceless automaton puts down the walkie-talkie and gives us a quick salute.

"Normally," he says, "I would be able to offer you a free flight or a new seat, but after September 11 . . ."

I see his nose slide around between his cheeks.

"It is wartime," he says and his ear becomes jowelly. "We're doing the best we can."

Dear Luddie,

Before it was wartime on September 11 I got up early so I could have breakfast at the Good Thyme Deli in New England.

When I got to the Good Thyme Deli in New England, I saw the old married owners of the deli arguing about tomatoes.

"Take these tomatoes to the storage room!" the wife yelled to her husband.

"I'll get to it," the husband grumbled.

"You'll never get to it!" the wife shrieked. "I want you to take them into the storage room and I want you to do it now!"

The husband grumbled something more as he took the tomatoes to the storage room, and his wife made a few more shrill declarations about him as he went.

When the door to the storage room slammed shut, the husband stopped grumbling and the wife stopped declaring, and I heard the tiny brown speaker above me broadcasting the news.

On the tiny brown speaker above me broadcasting the news, a man says that a plane crashed into the World Trade Center.

". . . like an axe flung into a birthday cake," the man on the radio says.

As I heard the man say that it was wartime, I thought about the prop plane that had crashed into the White House a few years before. I thought about the comical picture in the paper the next day. I saw the tail of the little plane sticking out of the small boxy window of the White House.

With the comical picture of the little plane sticking out of the small boxy window of the White House in my mind, I finished my breakfast and walked into the bright blue and black and yellow day of September 11.

On the bus, an old man in army fatigues and sunglasses said, "We're all fucked now!"

He shook his cane at me.

"We are all fucked!" he said again, looking around at everyone on the bus.

I wondered how we were all fucked if it was just a little prop plane with its tail sticking out.

Once I got to work and looked at a TV in the back room, I began to see how we were all fucked.

It was wartime like an axe flung into a birthday cake.

It was wartime and we were all fucked because this was not a little plane with its tail sticking out of the small boxy window of the White House. This was something blue and black and yellow and orange. This was something blue and black and orange and gray and strange and horrible and we were all fucked.

Outside the door of the back room, I saw a woman with a small plastic Buddha doll run to the self-help section.

She ran into the self-help section and she yelled at the Buddha doll, "Where are you? Where are you? Where are you?" but of course the Buddha doll didn't answer because something blue and orange and black and gray and strange and horrible had blown up the tall blocks that stuck New York to the sky.

It was wartime.

I wrote a letter to the Bombardier a day after the woman ran into the self-help section with her Buddha doll. I wrote a letter to the Bombardier when paper from the tall blocks still filled the sky, and I asked him what I should do. I asked him what I should do because something strange and horrible had happened and I needed to know what a young man in such a story should do.

My brother knew what to do. He joined the Marines. He joined the Marines, and he marched in time, and he shaved his head, and he called me up to tell me I had to do it too. All of it.

"It's wartime, baby bitch," he said, "In wartime, this is what we do. So suck it up little brother, and be a good soldier."

I asked the Bombardier in my letter, "What is a young man in wartime?"

I asked him, "Should a young man in wartime join the fight?"

I asked him because I had always thought a young man in such a story would leave for Canada if any American war needed him to die, but I also thought a young man in such a story would be a hero.

Now it seemed there would be an American war that needed young men to die, and I wasn't sure I wanted to leave for Canada because Canada seemed like a cold, mossy nest full of cowards.

Could a young man be a hero in Canada during wartime?

Could a young man be a hero and not kill?

After a few days, the Bombardier wrote back.

"I don't know what a young man is in wartime," he wrote, "In wartime, some young men join the fight and other young men don't. There are other ways to win the war. How you will win this war, I don't know, but I don't believe it will be by joining the fight. Your brother has joined the fight, and I pray for him."

After I got this letter, I celebrated.

It seemed I could maybe still be a hero and not join the fight during wartime. I didn't want to die, and I didn't want to kill, and I didn't want to be a baby bitch, so I found a place to live after all the paper from the tall blocks fell from the sky in New York, and I celebrated my not joining the fight.

This place to live was a rented row house in New England.

I lived there with Bernadette and our cats and our friends Big B and Medium B.

I became a hero for the cats.

I became a hero for the cats because I sat up nights in this place, smoking cigarettes and drinking wine.

Very often, I became a hero for the cats because I became Madame Psychosis and talked to them for hours and hours about the correspondences between the past and the present.

The cats loved this talk, and so they purred and rubbed against my legs.

I was a hero.

Dear Luddie,

Bernadette and I live gently in New England. We eat only vegetables in New England, and we love our two cats. At night in New England, I lie awake wondering whether or not I've locked the front door.

"Am I winning the war?" I wonder.

"No one lives gently enough," I say to myself and go downstairs to check on the front door.

After I check on the front door I feed the cats and smoke cigarettes and drink wine and become Madame Psychosis while Bernadette sleeps upstairs.

"No one lives gently enough," I say to the cats.

They purr and rub against my legs.

"He's not our president," I say to the cats. "No way."

Men in fatigues shake their canes at me and men in fatigues walk by me through the airport. He's their president and he's the president of the airline supervisor.

Bernadette and I walk away.

The men in fatigues walking through the airport look younger than me, and they walk through the sea of travelers in the airport as Bernadette and I wait for our new, much later flight to Frankfurt without the Bombardier.

These men younger than me in fatigues walk through the airport on their way to Fort Bragg, Fort Benning, and Fort Hood.

They walk on their way to Fort Bragg, Fort Benning, and Fort Hood, and then they will be off to Kabul, Kandahar, Kirkuk, Baghdad, or Tikrit in their fatigues.

They will not be gentle enough.

These men younger than me in fatigues will be fighting and dying in an American war that needs them to fight and die, but Bernadette and I will not fight and die in this American war.

We will not wear fatigues.

He's not our president.

If the faceless automatons at the airport ever let us, Bernadette and I will go to your country, Luddie. We won't fight and die in this American war for this president. We will go to your country instead and when we go to your country, Luddie, Bernadette and I will fight for the Bombardier.

Dear Luddie,

What do you believe makes history?

Do you believe stories make history?

Do you believe plot, setting, time, and characters make history?

The Bombardier believes.

The Bombardier believes stories make history, and the Bombardier believes history makes a story. It has a plot, a setting, time, and characters.

He believes these stories from history tell him something about the present.

What they tell him, I don't know, because he sometimes confuses the thoughts of history. He sometimes confuses the thoughts of the past with their present expressions, so the stories often tell him confusing things.

This confusion can make a great story, and it has always been wonderful to listen to the Bombardier tell the stories of history.

In his house, he has a library filled with the stories of history all waiting to be told by him in his clear voice.

It's a library full of green- and brown-spined books on shelves stretching up to the ceiling.

Once, when I was a boy and couldn't sleep, I wanted to hear one of these stories from history so badly I padded into the Bombardier's library where he sat at his desk poring over books.

I knew he would tell me a story even though it was late, because for weeks and weeks he had been reading stories from history, stories about his great ancestor, the Captain.

His head had been so full of stories then they fell from him freely. It never took much to get him to tell one, even if it was late at night, even if I was just a little boy.

"Well, good evening!" he said when I shuffled into the library in my footed pajamas, dragging my blanket.

"What can I do for you at this late hour, little man?" he asked, sipping his drink.

He had turned in his chair, draping one arm across the creaky wooden back.

"I can't sleep," I said. "Will you tell me a story?"

A child's ploy.

I climbed into a green leather chair beside the desk and pulled my blanket around me.

"I don't know if the stories I have are for little boys," the Bombardier said. "They're a little scary."

"I'm not scared of a story," I said. "You can tell me any story."

I was very tough.

"Hmm," the Bombardier said, removing his glasses and putting a stem in his mouth, "I'm just now reading a few stories about the Captain . . ."

"Yes!" I said, "Tell me a story about the Captain!"

"You won't get scared?" he asked, pointing his glasses at me. "You wouldn't rather hear Anderclese and the Lion? Or the story of Stan Musial?"

"Never," I said, thrusting out my little chin.

"Well then," the Bombardier said, smoothing my blanket out around me, "I'll tell you a story about the Captain."

This, I thought, would be very exciting.

"The Captain," the Bombardier began in a storytelling voice, "was a man from Old England, with big red sideburns, a big blue hat, and a sword."

"Like Cap'n Crunch?" I asked.

"Captain who?" the Bombardier said.

"Crunch!" I said, "Cap'n Crunch the cereal."

"Oh," the Bombardier said. He thought it over.

"I guess so. I guess you could say he was like Captain Crunch the cereal, but this Captain was a bit more than cereal. He had a real sword."

"Okay," I said, trying to picture this new captain with his blue hat, red sideburns, and sword.

"This story," the Bombardier said, "takes place a long time ago, when the Captain came to the New World from Old England."

He opened a green history book for me and pointed at a drawing of the New World. There were swords and naked men. Indians.

"The Captain came to the New World in 1630 on this ship with a man named John Winthrop and a few of what they called 'goodly women and men.'"

"Why?" I asked, staring at the naked Indians.

"Why what?" he said.

"Why did they call them 'goodly'?" I said.

The Bombardier smiled.

"Because they loved God very much," he said. "Now you need to listen to this story if you want me to tell it."

"Okay," I said, "but are you goodly?"

He thought for a second.

"Why," the Bombardier said, "I suppose I try to be."

"I can tell," I said, always trying to please.

"Thank you," the Bombardier said. "Now no more interruptions, or I will send you back to bed."

He waved the book at me.

"Right," I said, "no more interruptions."

"In this story," the Bombardier said, standing up, "the Captain came to the New World to protect this man named John Winthrop and the goodly women and men of New England.

"In this story, you see, the Captain was a brave soldier."

The Bombardier began to pace the floor, touching his fingertips to the book.

I could tell by the way the wrinkles on his face moved that this was going to be a big story. I wouldn't have to go to bed for a long time.

"But in other stories the Captain was not just a brave soldier," the Bombardier said, frowning, "In other stories the Captain was a bad man."

He stopped pacing and the wrinkles on his face pulled tight. He reached over and took a drink. After a second, the wrinkles went slack again.

"But in this story," the Bombardier said, pacing again, "the Captain was a brave soldier because he killed what was not goodly."

"I'm not scared," I said, because it seemed like we might be getting to a scary part.

"The Captain was a brave soldier," the Bombardier went on, "because evil savages at a place called Fort Mystic had killed two of the Captain's goodly fellows, an Englishman and a Dutchman."

The Bombardier held up two fingers and nodded at me to make sure I was listening to his story.

I was listening, so I held two fingers up back at him.

"These two, the Englishman and the Dutchman," the Bombardier went on, "were killed by evil Pequot savages."

He frowned.

"Pequots," he said, "are Indians in headdresses and deer skins, with face paint and arrows."

"Indians," I said, "savages."

"Right," he said, "and these Pequot savages not only killed these two fellows, but they taunted the other brave soldiers who had been the friends of these two fellows."

Here, the Bombardier's face screwed up into something terrible. The lines in his skin went all crazy. He pointed at me and stuck out his tongue.

"Taunted them about their dead friends," he said.

I nodded.

"We know this story," he said, louder now, "because the brave soldiers of the New World enjoyed telling their stories in books to the people of the Old World.

"This is what soldiers do."

He stopped pacing and looked at the book in his hand.

"One brave soldier who had settled in the New World told his story in a book to the people of the Old World," he said, opening the green-spined book, "and this story goes like this.

"'These Pequots,'" he read from the book in his clearest voice, "'came with their canoes into the River in View of the Soldiers within the Fort, and when they apprehended themselves out of reach of the Soldiers' guns, these Pequots would imitate the Dying Groans and Invocations of the poor Captive English, which the English Soldiers were forced with silent patience to bear, not being then in Capacity to requite their insolent blasphemies.

"'But the English Soldiers, being by these horrible Outrages justly provoked to Indignation, unanimously agreed to join their forces together to root them out of the Earth with God's Assistance.'"

"I know what blasphemy is," I said.

The Bombardier frowned.

"Oh yes?"

"Yes," I said, "it's when your Bible Pictionary team can't get your drawing of a mustard seed in Sunday school and you say G.D."

The Bombardier was quiet.

"Yes," he said finally, "and sometimes it's more. Sometimes it's more than saying G.D. and when it's more, you need a brave soldier to root out the blasphemers. Do you know any brave soldiers?"

"Cap'n Crunch!" I said.

"Hmm," the Bombardier said, "no."

I giggled and rubbed my feet together under my blanket.

I understood that to requite the insolent blasphemies of the Pequots, the governor of New England had sent the Captain, the Bombardier's great ancestor. I understood we were a family of brave soldiers.

"In this story," the Bombardier said, "the Governor of New England knows the Captain can root the Pequots out with God's assistance, because the Governor of New England knows the Captain is a brave soldier.

"He knows because by this time, the Captain has already gone to a place called Block Island, not to silently bear outrages, but to requite the insolent blasphemies of the Pequots. This is what soldiers do, so he went. But once there on Block Island, the Captain found no Pequots, only rows of corn and small houses and dogs.

"To requite the insolent blasphemies, then, the Captain had to burn the rows of corn and the small houses on Block Island. He had to kill the dogs."

The Bombardier frowned.

"He killed the dogs on Block Island?" I asked, picturing a giant wooden alphabet block—the green letter "G"—with howling, burning dogs running on its top.

It was not a good picture.

"Yes," the Bombardier said, "but they were evil dogs."

"Oh," I said.

In my mind the letter "G" floated on blue water.

A block island with flaming dogs on top, burning and sad.

"So," the Bombardier went on, "because the Captain had burned the rows of corn and the small houses, and because he had killed the evil dogs, the Governor of New England knew the Captain was prepared to further requite the insolent blasphemies at Fort Mystic, where the real Pequots lived.

"The insolent blasphemies at Fort Mystic were not so easily requited as the dogs of Block Island, but they were requited nonetheless when the Captain burned these insolent Pequots at Fort Mystic. He burned them alive. He crept up to their huts one winter morning when the moon was bright, and he and a few other brave soldiers set fire to their huts and burned them alive."

"This is a story from history?" I asked, wrinkling my nose.

"Yes," the Bombardier said, "and we know it because the Captain was very proud of it, and he told his story in a book to the people of the Old World. His story about this requiting was published in the Old World under the title *News from the New World.*

"Do you want to hear *News from the New World?*" the Bombardier asked. I didn't answer.

He opened up a new book and said, "*News from the New World* goes like this:

"'We had sufficient light from the word of God for our proceedings.'"

The Bombardier read this one sentence to me, and then closed the new book and put it back in his library.

The shelves towered above me in my little green chair. History.

It's true, Luddie, I had gotten a little confused and a little scared by this story, but it wasn't because of the story itself, but because of how the Bombardier became in telling it. This story made his face red. It made his wrinkles dance all crazy.

But, even though I was a little confused and a little scared, I understood this light from the word of God lit the Pequots and burned them alive. I understood the goodly women and men of New England felt protected by the Captain, the Bombardier's great-great-great-great-great-grandfather.

I understood, but I wasn't sure I wanted to hear more. It might have been time for bed.

"Another brave soldier," the Bombardier said, holding up another book, "told this same story in a book to the people of the Old World. He told about this light from the word of God burning the Pequots in Fort Mystic. Listen!"

He shook my arm.

"'The Captain resolved to set the huts on fire,'" he read, "'whereupon the Indians tried every means of escape, not succeeding in which they returned back to the flames, preferring to perish by the fire than to die by our hands. What was most wonderful is that among this vast collection of men, women, and children, not one was heard to cry or scream.'"

The Bombardier was yelling now. He shook his fist in the air.

"According to this story," the Bombardier said looking down at the book, quiet again, "the Captain had sufficient light from the word of God to burn this vast collection of men, women, and children who did not cry or scream as they burned, and because the Captain burned them with the light of God the goodly women and men of New England felt protected by the Captain in the New World."

The Bombardier leaned against the shelf in his library, a little out of breath, smiling at me.

I understood. The Captain was a brave soldier.

"So," I said, "why was the Captain a bad man?"

The Bombardier's face softened. Its lines went slack. He laughed a little.

"I'll tell you," he said, scooping me up out of the chair to take me back to bed, "but you will have to be a little older."

"No! No!" I squealed, "I'm not sleepy! I'm older! Tell me the rest!"

"What a brave little man you are," he said, "but that's enough story for tonight. I'll tell you more later."

"No," I squealed, "Put me down! I'll root you out! Goddamn! I'll root you out!"

Even though I was a blasphemer, the Bombardier just laughed and carried me back to bed where I fell asleep, dreaming of the Pequots burning alive.

Dear Luddie,

I'm older now, and I live in New England where the Captain was a brave soldier and a bad man.

I live with Bernadette, our cats, and our friends, and we try our best to be good. We try our best to live gently.

We're not brave soldiers.

I sit at our kitchen table and watch out the window as our neighbors dig vegetables from the ground and pedal their bicycles through the snow. I watch them hold hands and kiss as they hang their tattered clothes on a line.

These women, I think, watching them from the table, they live more gently than we do.

They have a banner strung across their porch that reads "No Blood for Oil," and they ride their bicycles through the snow, and they huddle together in the winter without oil heating them. They pull their clothes from dumpsters and hang them on the line, and they eat vegetables straight from the ground.

They do not trade blood for oil, Luddie. They love one another and they sit on their back steps holding hands and smoking joints, and they are gentle, gentle women, Luddie.

I watch them out the window, and then I walk from our warm kitchen through the snow to the library where I read about the Captain, but I think about our neighbors.

I think about our neighbors, and I read about the Captain, and it's true both my home and the library are heated by blood.

I'm warm in the library under the lights with a book in my hands reading about the Captain, that bad man and brave soldier from the past.

I'm warm at home as I think about our neighbors hanging their tattered clothes on the line.

In the warm library under the fluorescent lights, away from these gentle women, I read about the Captain. I read that the Captain was a bad man. He was a bad man because he was "hypocritical and licentious."

This is what I learn when I am older, when I have learned some new words besides "blasphemy" and "goddamn."

"Hypocritical."

"Licentious."

When I move to New England and read books in the warm New England libraries lit by blood, this is what I learn.

The Captain is a bad man, I read in the fluorescent light of a New England library, because the Captain is always "under a religious mask practicing evil."

This is what I learn from reading the story of John Winthrop, the great founder of New England where I live now beside the gentle women bound by the strength of love.

In John Winthrop's story, the Captain is a bad man because he practices evil under a religious mask on the ship over to the New World. He lectures the goodly women and men about the strength of love.

In John Winthrop's story, the strength of love and the light from the word of God can't build anything together but evil, so the Captain is a bad man.

I don't like John Winthrop's story when I read it in the fluorescent light of the New England library.

I liked the Captain's story that I had listened to that night in the Bombardier library.

I liked the Captain's story because it had a red-bearded Cap'n Crunch burning the enemy alive, but I can see now it wasn't the whole story. Once I read other stories I find in history books in New England, I know the story I had listened to was only a little part of a story from a larger history.

John Winthrop's story of the Captain's hypocrisy and licentiousness, I read, is "proved to the Captain's face by a sober, goodly woman, whom the Captain had seduced on the ship over to the New World."

In the larger history, the Captain is not just a brave soldier.

Killing dogs and burning Pequots is brave in the larger history, but seducing the goodly women of New England is not.

A sober, goodly woman proved the Captain was hypocritical and licentious, seducing goodly women, and it makes a bad story for the Captain.

It makes a bad story because the goodly women and men think the strength of love can kill as easily as the light of God, and so they live in fear of the Captain and his strong love.

I read that the Captain can't resist the strength of love, so he joins a bad crowd of strong lovers.

I read that he joins the bad crowd of a woman named Ann Hutchinson and a man named John Wheelwright, and he lectures on and on about the strength of love.

His love is strong, and he is not shy.

The Captain signs petitions and lectures the colonists about the strength of love.

This is what I learn.

In the Captain's time it's very bad of the Captain to forsake the light of God for the strength of love.

He is a bad man for doing it, but he doesn't stop.

I read in John Winthrop's story that the Captain, the bad man, is next "charged by a goodly young woman to have solicited her chastity under pretence of Christian love, and to have confessed to her that he had his will oftentimes of the cooper's wife, and all out of the strength of love."

Out of the strength of love, the Captain spends afternoons with this cooper's wife, a woman John Winthrop says was "young and beautiful and withal of a jovial spirit and behavior."

The Captain is a brave soldier, and he believes he knows about the strength of love.

He believes he knows about the strength of love, and he believes the strength of his love makes him a good man and goodly women should embrace his strong love.

In the Captain's story, the cooper's wife is of troubled mind and in need of the strength of love, so the Captain devotes himself to private prayer with her in her house, with the door locked from the inside.

In John Winthrop's story, in the larger history, this is not what a brave soldier should do but it is what brave soldiers do over and over again throughout the stories of history.

In John Winthrop's story, to pray with the cooper's wife with the door locked from the inside is evil.

The Captain, in John Winthrop's story, has moved nearly beyond forgiveness by the strength of his love.

He has moved nearly beyond forgiveness but John Winthrop can't requite his insolent blasphemies, because the Captain is a brave soldier as well as a bad man, and John Winthrop and the goodly women and men of New England need brave soldiers no matter how bad, no matter how strong their love.

The goodly men and women need brave soldiers, so they let the Captain stay, and they cower from the strength of his love.

Until finally the strength of his love overcomes even the need for brave soldiers and the Captain's story in New England ends. It ends like this:

"The next day he was called again and banished."

Dear Luddie,

The Captain was called again and banished to New Hampshire and to New Amsterdam where he lectured about the strength of love and the joys of tobacco.

He loved tobacco so he lectured about its joys, and he lectured about the strength of his love, and he put his strength and joy into practice without worldly consequence.

He lectured about the strength of love and the joys of tobacco, and he partook of both of them freely in New Hampshire and New Amsterdam while at the same time lighting evil savages with the word of God and spreading his story throughout the New World.

The strength of love and the joys of tobacco and smoke from the savages lit by the word of God carried the Captain's story over the New World, from New England to New Hampshire, from New Hampshire to New Amsterdam, from New Amsterdam to Pennsylvania, from Pennsylvania to Ohio, and from Ohio to Iowa, where the Bombardier read it in a book.

The Bombardier read this story in a green-spined book, and he believed this story made history because he read it in a book. He believed this history in this book had carried this story from man to man to him, and because of this history he believed himself destined to be some kind of brave soldier. Because of this history the Bombardier believed himself destined to be some kind of man.

Dear Luddie,

A story is a tree with roots that pull water from the soil to make branches and leaves. Birds and squirrels and spiders can live freely in the leafy branches of a story because of the water pulled from the soil by the roots.

After the birds and squirrels and spiders have lived freely in the leafy branches of the story for years and years, the story begins to rot.

What makes the story rot?

Time and insects make the story rot, and because the story rots the story dies. The story rots and dies and becomes a ghost full of insects and rot, but this is not sad. This is not sad, because when the story rots and dies and becomes a ghost full of insects it becomes a home for the woodpecker who flies to the ghostly story and steps on its ghostly wood.

The woodpecker flies to the ghostly story, steps on the ghostly wood, and sticks his beak down in the rotten, ghostly story to find the insects the story has made for him.

In the Captain's tree I am a woodpecker.

I am a woodpecker sucking the insects out of the ghostly wood, because the story is dead.

The story is dead but filled with juicy, flaming insects lit by the word of God.

Juicy, flaming insects do not fill the Bombardier's story, and so in the Bombardier's tree I am not a woodpecker. I am not a woodpecker, because the Bombardier's story is not dead.

In the Bombardier's tree I may be another kind of bird, or I may be a squirrel, or I may be a spider living in the branches surrounded by breathing green leaves.

A forest is full of stories and creatures living freely within the leafy branches of the stories.

In the Bombardier's story I may be another kind of bird, or I may be a squirrel, or I may be a spider living freely in the branches of a story, because the Bombardier's story is alive and growing, pulling water from the soil with its roots.

I may be a bird, a squirrel, or a spider, or I may be a little man sitting in the shadow of the story. I may be a little man staring up at the story, comparing it to a tree.

Dear Luddie,

The Captain sailed to the New World in a ship filled by the light of God. The light of God burned a clearing in the New World for the Old World to grow. By the burning light of God the Old World did indeed grow until it filled the New World with the burning light of God and the burning story of the Captain.

By 1944, the burning story of the Captain had grown by the burning light of God. The burning story of the Captain had grown so big in the New World by 1944 that it cast a shadow across the ocean onto the edges of the Old World.

From the edges of the Old World to its center, the Old World's story had begun to rot and fill with insects by 1944, so in 1944 the Bombardier flew in a plane with a belly full of bombs to burn the evil out from the old stories of the capitals of the Old World.

He flew to the rotten story full of insects like a yellow-bellied sapsucker flies to a rotten tree.

He had a bird's-eye view.

He surveys the story for the veins of evil insects. His neck muscles tense when he sees the veins full of evil insects and the sound of his precision echoes throughout the forest of stories.

Dear Luddie,

Bernadette and I finally fly to the Old World in the shadow of the Bombardier's story.

Finally.

We finally get on a plane and leave Chicago to fly over the ocean to the Old World. Even though we fly to the Old World thousands of feet in the air, sixty years after his story, we still fly in its shadow.

As I sit on the plane in my blue seat, I wonder if soon, no plane will be able to fly free from the shadows of the Bombardier's story because of time and insects.

Once time and insects kill the Bombardier's story, will the Bombardier's story finally and forever tower above all planes?

Above every seat, will a more storied seat cast a shadowy spell?

Above every window, will a more storied window distort the view of the clouds?

Above every cloud will there hover another, more storied cloud?

This final and forever casting of shadowy spells?

Will it happen soon, I wonder.

A light from the wing of our plane flying to the Old World echoes through the clouds over the Atlantic Ocean, and the light hits a cloud that casts a shadow.

The lit cloud casts a shadow, but it is not a shadow from the Bombardier's story because that final and forever casting hasn't yet happened.

The casting hasn't happened, so this shadow is a shadow from my own story.

A light from a plane flashed through the clouds once when I was a boy.

It cast a shadow and made a story.

The story is that I stared up at this flashing light with my brother.

We had been throwing a ball back and forth on a field, but we got bored. We were boys, so we got bored.

When we got bored, we sprawled out on the grass with our baseball gloves behind our heads and we stared up at the sky.

This was before we had killed the hermit crabs, before we had ever heard of Madame Psychosis, and before I held a gun to his head and pulled the trigger.

"Look at that cloud," my brother said. "A light from a plane just flashed through it."

I squinted up at the sky.

"It looks like your face that time Roy threw you against the wall," I said.

"Roy never threw me against the wall," my brother said.

"Yes," I said, "he did. You wanted a snack, strawberry yogurt I think, and he told you to go back to bed, but you wouldn't. You were seven or eight, probably. You stood there, maybe you stamped your foot. I don't know. But you yelled, 'I want strawberry-banana yogurt!' and he grabbed you around the shoulders and threw you at the bed, but you went past the bed and hit the wall. It was funny to watch. Your face. It was so funny."

I was laughing now.

"I remember," I said, "because Roy laughed after you hit the wall and fell back on the bed. He laughed and then he looked at me with the weirdest face. He said, 'Child abuse is easy,' and then he left like he always did."

"Roy never had the weirdest face," my brother said.

He wouldn't look at me.

His face had turned away.

"You're thinking of *Tales of a Fourth Grade Nothing,*" he said, "or that Iron Maiden song, 'Seventh Son.'"

We both looked up at the cloud the light had passed through again.

"That cloud looks like you getting punched in the nuts," he said.

"Oh," I said.

He was older.

"I'm going back home, loser," he said.

He got up and threw his glove at my face.

"Oh," I said, looking at the cloud again.

Dear Luddie,

Mr. B-17 was only twenty-four years old when the Bombardier's plane came to him in a dream. It came to him in a dream, and it cast a chrome shadow over his twenty-four-year-old brain.

This sounds like a good story, doesn't it?

Well, it is a good story, Luddie, so read it carefully, because it's time to tell it up here in the plane with Bernadette on our way to the Old World.

In this story, just before Mr. B-17 fell asleep one night, Mr. B-17 had let his mind linger on the tangy, sweet taste of his wife's hatpins. Mr. B-17 and his wife had come home drunk from a cocktail party that night, and Mr. B-17 had pulled his wife's hatpins out of her hair with his teeth, slowly and gently before kissing her good night on the head. He had let his mind linger on the tangy, sweet taste of these hatpins, and then he fell asleep.

While Mr. B-17 was asleep, the Bombardier's plane flew to him in a dream.

He awoke from the dream. He showered, shaved, and then he ate two pieces of bacon his wife had cooked for him. He ate the bacon, and then he carried the chrome-shadowed dream into an office in the Midwest where, in between cups of coffee and Lucky Strikes, he transposed this chrome-shadowed dream into lines on paper.

After he transposed his dream into lines on paper, he went out for pie.

When he went out for pie, he dropped his lines on paper off at the Office of the Makers.

The Office of the Makers took these lines on paper and, after several months, transposed them into metal, rubber, glass, and glue.

This metal, rubber, glass, and glue became the Flying Fortress, the B-17 Bomber.

Mr. B-17 and his wife went out to the airfield to see this Flying Fortress months later when it had finally been made. When he saw the

Flying Fortress shining in the sun, Mr. B-17 kissed his wife on the top of her hatless head.

"What will it do?" his wife asked him.

"It will drop bombs on the Old World," he said.

"What Old World?" she asked and a gust of wind blew across the plains.

The gust of wind sent one of the propellers of the Flying Fortress spinning, and then it blew Mr. B-17's wife's hair into her eyes.

"Oh," she said, reaching up, "why didn't I wear a hat?"

Mr. B-17 looked down at her and smiled, feeling that life was full of codes made just for him to decipher.

All around them, the Makers scurried in their white shirtsleeves.

The transposition of a dream into metal, rubber, glass, and glue excited the Makers so much, they scurried always around everything. They scurried and stood by the turret guns. They scurried and stood by the four propellers. They scurried and stood by the bomb-bay doors and the little glass bubble in the nose of the Flying Fortress.

They scurried and stood by these things in their white shirtsleeves, and they posed. They stood and posed while photographers recorded their poses for history.

They had built a Flying Fortress from a dream, metal, rubber, glass, and glue, and this Flying Fortress would become part of the Arsenal of Democracy, dropping thousand-pound bombs on the Old World.

These Flying Fortresses in the Arsenal of Democracy reached 104 feet across. These Flying Fortresses in the Arsenal of Democracy reached 75 feet from top to tail. These Flying Fortresses in the Arsenal of Democracy were sleek, chrome, and massive, with glass bubbles in their very tips.

In one of these glass bubbles the Bombardier would sit in 1944.

In 1944, he would peer down through the clouds to the snowy forests of the Old World. He would sit and peer down through the clouds, and he would open the bomb-bay doors when the snowy forests turned to steel buildings.

The Bombardier would open the bomb-bay doors, and then he would release the thousand-pound bombs.

The thousand-pound bombs would fall through the clouds and land on the snowy ground and in the steel buildings.

The thousand-pound bombs would set the Old World on fire, and from his glass bubble in the Flying Fortress the Bombardier would watch the Old World burn.

He would be higher in the sky than anyone in his family had ever been, but he would not be alone.

Young men like the Bombardier would fly higher in the sky than anyone in their families had ever flown because of the Flying Fortresses.

They would all fly together, and they would watch the Old World burn, and they would sing this song:

Off we go
Into the wild blue yonder,
Climbing high
Into the sun.

Dear Luddie,

Bernadette and I are in the wild blue yonder. We are in the sky, but no one sings, they just watch TV or sleep.

I do not watch TV or sleep, I look out the window at the wild blue yonder and the clouds, and I think of stories. I think of my story, and I think of Mr. B-17's story, and I think of the radical daughter's story too.

She has another story besides the Bombardier's story.

Her story is that she won't go into the wild blue yonder.

Her story is a pretty good one, though very different from Mr. B-17's or the Bombardier's story. Her story is more like my story and so I'm going to tell it to you up here in the wild blue yonder, Luddie.

The radical daughter won't go into the sky because the one time she did, everyone around her had a red or a blue face.

Everyone had a red or a blue face, and these faces terrified her.

She didn't want to go into the wild blue yonder even the one time she did, but the man she was married to made her go into the sky and fly from the South to the Midwest. He made her fly from the South to the Midwest with him so they could make thousands of dollars.

They could make thousands of dollars, because he had filled his shoes with cocaine.

He had filled his shoes with cocaine in the South, and if they flew to the Midwest quickly, he could deliver the cocaine-filled shoes to someone who would give him thousands of dollars for them.

The wild blue yonder did not terrify the man the radical daughter was married to.

The wild blue yonder was his friend, because the wild blue yonder helped him deliver cocaine-filled shoes to the Midwest quickly, and when he did this, he made thousands of dollars.

He thought the wild blue yonder was very friendly.

Lately, though, the wild blue yonder had become less and less friendly.

The man she was married to had liked the wild blue yonder less and less lately, because lately the faceless automatons in the sky had been harassing him.

The faceless automatons in the sky had been harassing him because he had long hair and a beard. They had been harassing him because he had a leather jacket and torn jeans, because he was a long-haired man with a beard in a leather jacket and torn jeans who might be trying to deliver cocaine-filled shoes to someone in the Midwest.

The man she was married to decided this harassment had to stop, so he cut his hair and he shaved his beard. He cut his hair, shaved his beard, bought a suit, and filled his shoes with cocaine. He cut his hair, shaved his beard, bought a suit, filled his shoes with cocaine, and made his wife and baby fly into the wild blue yonder with him.

Surely the faceless automatons in the sky would not harass such a family man.

Surely they would not suspect such a family man of delivering cocaine-filled shoes to the Midwest.

Surely, he thought, this is a great plan.

It was a great plan, but the radical daughter didn't want to do it.

She didn't want to do it because she got vertigo, she said.

She was terrified, she said, of the wild blue yonder.

"Bullshit," the man she was married to said, and loaded her up with yellow pills.

Off they went, loaded with yellow pills and cocaine-filled shoes, into the wild blue yonder, and because it was a great plan no one harassed them.

No one harassed them, but halfway through the flight through the wild blue yonder, the baby boy began to wail.

The baby boy wailing was not part of the great plan.

Halfway through the flight the baby boy began to wail, and the cocaine began to spill out of the shoes.

Up in the sky, the man she was married to tried to hush the baby boy.

Up in the sky, the man she was married to secretly snorted the spilled cocaine.

Up in the sky, the man she was married to poked her, but she was loaded up with yellow pills, so she just smiled.

She smiled because her baby boy fit so nicely in her lap.

She drifted into sedation and looked at the clouds out the window, thinking her baby boy was flying so pleasantly, but really the pressure on his ears was making him wail.

His wailing was pleasant to the heavily sedated radical daughter, like a distant ambulance on a summer night in a big, radical city.

The man she was married to had such a nice red face.

It kept coming in close to her face and making soft whispery noises.

"Off we go," she sang, "into the wild blue yonder.

"Climbing high," she sang, "into the sun."

Then, the yellow pills wore off.

Then, the baby boy was still wailing.

Then, the baby boy was blue in the face.

Then, the other passengers were not wailing with blue faces.

Then, they were staring at her with red faces.

Then, the man she was married to stared at her with the reddest face of all, and he kept scooping cocaine from his shoe and snorting it.

The radical daughter looked out the window into the wild blue yonder and became terrified.

Off we go into the wild blue yonder.
Climbing high into the sun.

When the plane finally came down out of the wild blue yonder, the radical daughter and the man she was married to ran off the plane with their baby boy and their red faces and their cocaine and sweat pouring everywhere.

They ran off the plane and delivered the shoes and got the thousands of dollars, but the radical daughter never got on a plane again. No way.

She made the man she was married to use the thousands of dollars to fly himself back down to the South and to buy a truck. She made him use the thousands of dollars to load their couch and bed into the truck and to move their couch and bed back up to the Midwest where she said she would be waiting with her baby boy if the man promised not to fill his shoes with cocaine ever again.

The man she was married to used the thousands of dollars to fly back down to the South, and to buy a truck, and to load their couch and bed into the truck, and to move back up to the Midwest to be with her.

The man she was married to promised not to fill his shoes with cocaine ever again, and so they lived together in the Midwest.

They had another baby boy in the Midwest, me, but because the man she was married to was not a keeper of promises, she did not stay married to him long. Soon, he flew off into the wild blue yonder again with his shoes filled with cocaine, and he never came back.

Dear Luddie,

Let me tell you what Bernadette and I do in Frankfurt, Germany when we get off the plane.

When Bernadette and I get off the plane in Frankfurt, Germany, we stretch.

When Bernadette and I get off the plane in Frankfurt, Germany, after two days of waiting and flying and not sleeping, we stretch and we smile at each other.

I feel tired and also psychotic, but I follow smiling Bernadette to the passport line without making any psychotic scenes.

My eyebrows are big bags of water waiting to burst over my eyes.

My feet are sweaty.

In Frankfurt, Germany the passport line does not move.

In Frankfurt, Germany a huge family stands behind us in the line, speaking loudly in French. The mother smells like cocoa butter and sweat, and she jiggles a small chubby baby in her arms.

She jiggles the baby. The line moves. Slowly.

In Frankfurt, Germany we stand in this line with the jiggling baby just long enough to miss our flight to Berlin.

The light in the airport, I notice, in Frankfurt, Germany, makes everyone look like ugly, yellow ghosts.

In Frankfurt, Germany we shuffle into the yellow basement to try to find another ugly flight to Berlin. Surrounded by this ugly yellow ghost light, we find a faceless automaton who types on her computer.

We lean wearily on the counter, half-expecting our bodies to fall through the surface, but we are solid, and the faceless automaton hands us tickets for a later flight, but she does not smile.

She is a German faceless automaton.

We are in Frankfurt, Germany now, and in Frankfurt, Germany, we wait.

Dear Luddie,

In Frankfurt, Germany we wait, and then we board the plane to Berlin.

In Frankfurt, Germany we board the plane to Berlin, but the plane to Berlin does not take off.

"Communications problems," the German pilot said in English in Frankfurt, Germany.

Where is the Bombardier?

The Bombardier, as far as we know, waits in Berlin.

He waits for us alone in Berlin with his stories.

Bernadette has closed her eyes and rested her forehead on the seat in front of her on this new, unmoving plane.

Let me ask you a question, Luddie.

Is there such a thing as German efficiency, or have we misunderstood?

Is it part of a fable that simply does not translate into English?

In my tired and nervous state, I have felt flashes of panic at the inefficient, bureaucratic machinations of the Germans.

I have wondered if the fabled efficiency only begins when undesirable or unlisted people must be summarily rounded up for removal by face-less automatons.

We seem undesirable, and we are very close to unlisted, so I have felt flashes of panic.

I have felt flashes of panic, but we do not get rounded up by faceless automatons.

Instead, we sit, and we wait.

As I sit, waiting, the flashes of panic rise up and then subside.

After the flashes of panic subside, bolts of hot hatred for the German func-tionaries accomplishing nothing bubble up and sear my tender, tired insides.

These Germans are somehow worse even than the faceless automa-tons in Chicago, I think.

In a bolt of hot hatred, I want to splatter them all against the walls like flies.

I want to splatter all these Germans against the walls like fat, juicy horseflies and would I be a hero then?

What would history say?

Maybe you have felt this weird feeling bolt through you, or maybe you have felt very different, more complicated things about the Germans because of your history.

For now, in my story, you share my hatred, and maybe you see a correspondence with your own story from sixty years ago, though probably not.

The airplane is not a concentration camp.

Dear Luddie,

When I was a boy in history class my teacher said Berlin was the Bear City of the Old World.

I liked history, but I didn't like my teacher, so I never listened to him when he talked about history.

My teacher was so old he had taught the radical daughter history when she was a kid too.

When she was a kid, the radical daughter didn't listen to my teacher either.

The radical daughter told me that instead of listening to my teacher, she called him "Nigger Lips" and talked about boys with her friends.

She told me this and laughed.

This was not a word we used at my school, in my house, ever, so when the radical daughter said my teacher had "nigger lips" I felt the air turn sour in my lungs. I wanted to be a good boy, but there I was thinking of this terrible word all the time now afterwards.

I didn't use this word ever, but I didn't listen to him when he talked about history anymore either.

I just watched his lips.

Holy shit, I thought.

I watched his lips without listening to the words they made.

I watched his lips curling in on themselves and then popping out, tucking under the top teeth, then resting in an open pucker.

Don't think of the word, I thought. Don't think of it.

"Berlin, the Bear City of the Old World," my teacher's lips said.

Berlin, the city of swastikas and rubble, had also been filled with bears. Don't think of that word, please.

My teacher's lips said, "Berlin, the Bear City of the Old World," and then they said something else, but I didn't listen.

I was a kid and I was filled with dread in history class, so all I needed was to watch my teacher's lips without listening to the words they made, and my imagination created a city of swastikas and rubble and bears, so I wouldn't think of that word, and the radical daughter saying it and laughing.

I was almost Madame Pyschosis then.

Ever since this history class, no matter what history tells or doesn't tell with its lips, I see Berlin as a city full of bears in December of 1944.

Dear Luddie,

History tells us that by December of 1944, the Flying Fortresses had begun to destroy Berlin, the Bear City of the Old World.

The Flying Fortresses destroyed Berlin by dropping thousand-pound bombs on its buildings and its people every day and every night.

History tells us no punishment was too severe for the Arsenal of Democracy to inflict upon Berlin, no fire too great, because the Arsenal of Democracy not only had sufficient light from the word of God for its actions, it had a fleet of Flying Fortresses and thousand-pound bombs to perform them.

History tells us that by December of 1944, the Makers in their white shirtsleeves and the Dreamers with their hatpin mouths had made and dreamed of such destructive force that nothing short of total annihilation seemed fit or just for Berlin.

Nothing short of total annihilation seemed fit or just for Berlin, and nothing seemed fit or just for their dreams and their makings but the total annihilation of Berlin, so the Arsenal of Democracy dropped thousand-pound bombs on the buildings and the people of Berlin every day and every night.

History tells us that Berlin, even in December of 1944, still had been filled with buildings and people and red flags with black swastikas in their centers.

History tells us that these red flags with black swastikas in their centers had to be destroyed along with the buildings and people of Berlin so, history tells us, the Arsenal of Democracy dropped thousand-pound bombs on Berlin every day and every night.

Berlin and its buildings and its people were destroyed by the Arsenal of Democracy, history tells us, but what about the bears?

Were the bears destroyed by thousand-pound bombs?

History doesn't tell us anything about the bears, or how they were destroyed, but history tells us Berlin was the Bear City of the Old World, right?

That's what my teacher said. I watched him say it.

History tells us Berlin was the Bear City of the Old World, but history doesn't need to tell us Berlin is no longer the Bear City, because we can see on TV Berlin has no bears.

No bears at the wall.

No bears at the Reichstag.

History doesn't tell us about the bears, I think, because when the thousand-pound bombs dropped on Berlin in December of 1944, the thousand-pound bombs destroyed the bears completely.

You see, Luddie, history has forgotten about the bears because the bombs burned them up so completely.

The thousand-pound bombs destroyed the bears so completely no record of these bears exists.

No singed coat or ashy talon lay in the rubble for anyone to connect the bear-filled past of Berlin with the bear-less present after the thousand-pound bombs dropped, so the bears of Berlin have been forgotten by history.

History has turned them completely into ghosts, mouthed silently but not heard.

History has turned the bears into ghosts, but we can talk about these bears, Luddie, because we know about history and ghosts.

We know about bears.

We know that if you mouth the words without saying them, they still enter the world as ghosts of themselves, and ghosts still have meanings if not bodies.

Dear Luddie,

Listen to this history.

Berlin had been filled with bears in December of 1944.

I know it.

Bears foraging for meals in the Tiergarten, bears playing in the rubble of old churches, bears sleeping in abandoned bathtubs.

These foraging, playing, and sleeping bears burned.

They burned by the lights of God and democracy, along with the red flags with black swastikas in their centers. They burned along with the buildings and the people. The bears burned completely away when the Arsenal of Democracy dropped thousand-pound bombs on Berlin.

Dear Luddie,

We know how bears burn, Luddie, because the lights of God and democracy seek out bears to burn, but rarely do these burning bear stories get told in history.

I know only one story about burning bears from history, and I think it's important that I tell it to you.

It's a story from American history.

It's one of the stories of sailing and burning the explorers told when they sailed and burned their way through the New World and into American history.

It's another story the Bombardier told me when I was a boy, like the Captain's story.

When I was a boy, the Bombardier would read aloud from a book of stories as I settled into bed, letting the cold sheets slide on my little legs.

"Will you ever go to sleep?" the Bombardier asked me from his chair beside the bed, ice rattling in his glass.

"Never," I said.

"Hmm," he said, flipping through the pages of his book.

"I will stay up forever and become a tornado," I said, thrusting my little fist in the air.

I loved the tornado. Its destructive power. The train sound. Then nothing. You're dead.

"A tornado?" the Bombardier asked, opening the book.

"A tornado never sleeps," I said.

"Well, how about I read this tornado a little bit from my book?" he said.

"Okay," I said, "but I'll never sleep."

"Okay," he said, and began to read from his book.

"'About 5 p.m. my attention was struck,'" the Bombardier read, "'by one of the party running at a distance toward us and making signs and hollering as if in distress. I ordered the pirogues to put to, and waited until he arrived.'"

The story went like this, Luddie, with the Bombardier reading it to me in these long sentences with strange words, and I listened.

I listened because it's history, and it's important.

It makes a story.

I would never sleep.

"'I now found that it was Bratton,'" the Bombardier read, "'the man with the sore hand whom I had permitted to walk on shore. He arrived so much out of breath that it was several minutes before he could tell what had happened. At length he informed me that in the woody bottom on the lanyard side about one-and-a-half miles below us he had shot a brown bear, which immediately turned on him and pursued him a considerable distance, but he had wounded it so badly that it could not overtake him.'"

The Bombardier read this story to me in a kind of low voice, because I was a boy and liked to hear stories with voices.

"'I immediately turned out with seven of the party in quest of this monster,'" he read, "'We at length found his trail and pursued him about a mile by the blood through very thick brush of rosebushes and the large-leaved willow.

"'We finally found him concealed in some very thick brush and shot him through the skull with two balls.

"'We proceeded to dress him as soon as possible, we found him in good order. It was a monstrous beast, not quite so large as that we killed a few days past but in all other respects much the same. The hair is remarkably long, fine, and rich, though he appears partially to have discharged his winter coat.

"'We now found that Bratton had shot him through the center of the lungs, notwithstanding which he had pursued him near half a mile and had returned more than double that distance and with his talons had prepared himself a bed in the earth of about two feet deep and five long and was perfectly alive when we found him, which could not have been less than two hours after he received the wound.

"'These bear being so hard to die rather intimidates us all.

"'I must confess that I do not like the gentlemen and had rather fight two Indians than one bear. There is no other chance to conquer them by a single shot but by shooting them through the brains, and this becomes difficult in consequence of two large muscles which cover the sides of the forehead and the sharp projection of the center of the frontal bone, which is also of a pretty good thickness.

"'The fleece and skin were as much as two men could possibly carry.

"'By the time we returned the sun had set and I determined to remain here all night, and directed the cooks to render the bear's oil and put it in the kegs, which was done. There was about eight gallons of it.

"'We cooked the bear in its oil and we ate it.'"

Dear Luddie,

The Bombardier read me this story when I was a boy and I fell asleep dreaming of a soft bed with a dying bear in it.

I fell asleep and dreamt of burning bear meat.

Years later, when I wasn't a boy anymore, I read this story about the burning of a bear in America, sitting up in my tent in South Dakota, on my way to Oregon.

I was driving across the country with only a tent and some beans, and when I left the Midwest the Bombardier gave me this book of stories.

"I used to read it to you at bedtime," he said, patting me on my newly shaved head, "when you were a boy and wanted to be a tornado."

I didn't remember.

I didn't remember, so when I read this story again in my tent, with my shaved head and my can of beans, I didn't fall asleep.

I didn't fall asleep because it's a horrible story.

It's a horrible story, and I cried.

I cried for the bear preparing a bed for himself to die in.

I cried for the bear preparing his bed, because I thought the bear had been shot through the center of the lungs and in the brain for me.

He had been shot through the center of the lungs and in the brain so that I could drive through South Dakota to Oregon with no fear of bears or Indians.

I thought, this bear in the story had been shot through the center of the lungs and the brain so that I could drive through South Dakota to Oregon, so that I could buy bug repellent at Wal-Mart in Wyoming, and so that I could eat a burrito in Idaho with no fear of bears or Indians.

I wasn't a boy anymore, Luddie, but I wasn't quite a man, and I had set to no pirogues. I had no lanyard side. I just had my junky car, my shaved head, my beans, and my book of horrible stories.

This poor bear in this horrible story dug his deathbed with his talons as the blood filled his lungs and he waited for two shots to fill his brain, I thought, so that I could eat my burrito, and so my friends could eat their burritos, and so all of America could buy bug repellent from Wal-Mart.

Years after I was a boy in bed, I cried when I read this story because it is a martyr's story. The martyr bears died so that we could live.

These are the stories of history.

I cried when I read this martyr story from history, and I called the Bombardier from a payphone and asked him about the bears and shots and the Captain. I was older, so I asked if the Captain was really a bad man.

I asked the Bombardier about the Captain's story, and when he said it's true about the collection of men, women, and children quietly feeling the flames of the word of God burning them alive, I cried some more.

"Be brave," he said.

I tried to be brave, but I cried for the quiet men, women, and children because they had been burned alive so that I could watch people on TV and worry about the cats but nothing else. Everything had died so that I could live my stupid life.

Now that I am older, I know that crying about everything that has died is not enough, but now that I am older, I also know that crying is an accomplishment.

Crying is an accomplishment because time crumples when you cry.

Now that I am older, I know this is an accomplishment, like pulling a trigger.

I cried about the bears and the Pequots and felt like I had done something with my time.

I felt like I knew my history.

The bears and the Pequots had died so that I could eat burritos and buy things at Wal-Mart, and I had cried about it.

That was my history.

Dear Luddie,

The Bombardier and his fellow soldiers were a story from history in 1944. They were a story from history gazing out of their glass bubbles onto the burning ground of the Old World below them as it howled with bloody lungs in retreat. They were a story from history watching the bear city prepare its bed in the earth with its talons.

Who would be the martyr?

Who would live?

Berlin the Bear City was perfectly alive though wounded when it was sentenced to destruction by thousand-pound bombs in this story. It was perfectly alive, but with its talons it prepared itself a bed in the earth as the bombs fell down upon it, putting holes in its lungs, aiming for its brain.

Berlin the Bear City prepared a bed and let the ghosts rise up through the earth and the bombs fall down through the sky. It prepared a bed and let the ghosts rise and the bombs fall until the Allies finally caught up to it and shot it through the skull with two balls, and it died.

Berlin the Bear City died and became a city of broken correspondents.

Berlin the Bear City became a city of broken correspondents because through it ghosts shuffled, trying to reach the living. The living shuffled through the rubble of this ghostly correspondent, bear-skull city, but the living weren't sure if they were living, or if they were ghosts.

The living saw ghosts, and the ghosts saw the winter coat of the bear city partially discharged.

What had they died for?

The living drained the ghost oil from the bear city and marveled at the quantity.

The living felt weird and white and stumbled through the rubble of the cracked bear-skull city.

These were the Germans, Luddie, not dead but removed from the flesh of their lives, only able to feel the flesh of their lives through the dead body of their bear city, but dimly.

There were no singed bear coats or ashy bear talons in the rubble, but there were these people. These people cooked and ate the bear meat. Once they cooked the bear meat in bear oil and ate the bear meat cooked in bear oil, they dutifully made babies like good living German citizens of a bear city, but even when they made babies they hardly felt the flesh of their lives.

They dutifully but dully made babies because they knew they would shortly die if they hadn't died already, and making babies was all the half dead could do if they didn't want to become as completely extinct and ghostly as the bears that had run through Berlin only a few days before.

The German citizens made babies with the small hope somewhere dimly moving through their fleshless lives that one of these newly made babies might grow up to rebuild their bear city. They had this one small hope, but they were unsure whether this new bear city would be in the land of the living or the land of the dead.

Dear Luddie,

Flying into Berlin, Bernadette and I can feel the ghostly bear oil hovering between the new buildings built by hopeful babies.

We can feel the ghostly bear oil coating the grass like dew.

We can feel the ghostly bear oil in the morning haze, but we aren't sure if we are in the land of the living or the land of the dead.

We are tired and our lungs are leaking, but we have made it to this city alive.

Alive, we will find the Bombardier in his hotel, and we will walk through the land of the living and the land of the dead in Germany and in Poland, but only if we can stay awake and not drift back into more stories or clouds.

We have come down out of the stories and clouds and into Berlin, and in Berlin we must stay awake.

We must stay awake and not drift back into more stories or more clouds, because out of the sky and into Berlin, I know I've been a fool in these last letters to you.

I've been a fool in these last letters to you because I've written on and on about bears and flying fortresses and cocaine-filled shoes. I've written on and on about bears and flying fortresses and cocaine-filled shoes, but I haven't told you anything.

Here on the ground in Berlin, bears, flying fortresses, and cocaine-filled shoes tell us nothing.

Cabs, lunch, and hotels are so much more important than bears, flying fortresses, or cocaine-filled shoes, but I haven't thought about cabs, lunch, or hotels.

Here on the ground, I know I must think about cabs, lunch, and hotels and Bernadette and I must leave the bears, the flying fortresses, and the cocaine-filled shoes in the sky with the clouds.

We must leave them in the sky with the clouds, and we must take a cab to the hotel to find the Bombardier, and then we must eat and rent a car to drive to your country.

We are on the ground now.

On the ground, we will take a cab, find the Bombardier, and we will eat in this city. We will leave the bears, the flying fortresses, and the cocaine-filled shoes up there in the wild blue yonder with the clouds and the stories.

Dear Luddie,

We took a cab to the hotel, and we found the Bombardier here in Berlin.

He hadn't left his hotel.

When we found the Bombardier in his hotel he said, "Oh I'm so glad!" and he hugged us both.

The Bombardier hugged us both, and we smelled his green aftershave and felt his wool suit scratch against our tired and greasy skin.

When his wool suit scratched against my tired and greasy skin, I thought, "No one has been harmed, and no one has been lost."

I felt like crying, but I didn't want to crumple time.

When his wool suit scratched against my tired and greasy skin, I thought, "The time of our story hasn't even started yet."

"The time of our story will not crumple," I thought.

"Did you take a cab here to the hotel?" the Bombardier asked.

We nodded.

"When can we eat?" he asked.

Dear Luddie,

The only thing you need to know now is that our car is a Renault.

Forget the stories, forget the histories, there is only that our car is a black, boxy Renault with four doors, a radio, window shades, power locks, and a sunroof.

There is only this black, boxy Renault speeding down the Autobahn toward your country.

Forget Mr. B-17. Forget the bears. Forget the clouds over the fields. Forget the cocaine-filled shoes, the airline, and the Midwest.

Forget everything.

The only thing you need to know is that this Renault is a black box speeding down the Autobahn toward your country, and I'm driving it.

The only thing you need to know is that Bernadette sits in the passenger seat with the maps from the rental company, and the Bombardier sits in the backseat of the Renault with his hands folded in his lap.

The only thing you need to know is the Bombardier looks out the window of the Renault, first at Berlin, then at the fat German forests blurring by.

We made it out of the city of Berlin with its careening cars and changing streets. We made it onto the Autobahn, and now we're speeding toward your country in a black, boxy Renault.

The only thing you need to know is that the streets went in straight lines from one direction to the next. Bernadette navigated us through them with our cheap rental road map. We made it out onto the Autobahn.

We made it out on the Autobahn, but it was a struggle. The Bombardier sits in the backseat with his hands folded in his lap as our black box speeds down the Autobahn toward your country.

This is the only thing you need to know.

Dear Luddie,

On long car trips when we were kids, my brother and I would stretch our arms out to be the first in a new state. This is nothing special. Kids' stuff. From the backseat we'd push our fingers out and strain against our seat belts trying to be the first across the border into Illinois, Kentucky, Tennessee, Georgia, Florida.

Straining and giggling in the backseat.

That's how we crossed borders then, but now we do it differently. My brother—across states, countries, and continents—calls me on a shaky line from somewhere private.

"I fucking love it," he says, "To cross a border in a tank, with a rifle on my back, it's like being baptized."

He says, "The first time I did it, I jumped off the tank and ran back to the other side just to do it again, just so I could crawl across the border this time, just so I could feel that hot sand grinding under me. I wiped the line out with my belly, you know, gun on my back, the sun in my ears, an army behind me . . ."

"What," I ask, "border did you wipe out with your belly?"

"Sorry, buddy," he says. "Classified."

Crossing your border, Luddie, is not like being baptized. We do not get out of the car to do it again on our bellies. We do not have an army behind us.

Instead, we feel the clean, immaculate Autobahn crumble into a two-lane highway as we cross the muddy Oder River.

The border guard hardly looks at us and waves at us and then we are in your country.

We are in Poland.

When I imagined your country, Luddie, I imagined wild boars running through green forests, bearded men in orange armor, Vodka and flushed cheeks, dirty snow, feral cats, graffiti. Warsaw a gray Gotham, Krakow an immense library, Gdańsk a ruddy oyster. "Poland," my brother says, "Full of Polacks, I bet." Then he laughs. In my country, Luddie, we have names for everything.

Dear Luddie,

In your country our black, boxy Renault cannot speed on the bumpy two-lane highway. It can only lurch and jolt along as tiny Polish cars speed past on both sides of the road.

Tiny Polish cars speeding past on both sides of the road are new things to know. They have new names.

Giant Polish trucks are also new things to know.

Giant Polish trucks and tiny Polish cars are new things to know in a new story with new names.

Bernadette, the Bombardier, and I have come from the Autobahn into a new story on this bumpy, two-lane highway in your country, and this new story has new things to know.

Dear Luddie,

In your country, I would like to transport these new things—these giant Polish trucks and tiny Polish cars, this bumpy two-lane road—in their new story to you, Luddie, but to transport these giant Polish trucks and tiny Polish cars in their new story to you, I would need your language.

I would need your language to transport these giant Polish trucks and tiny Polish cars, to make their impossible swerving real, to make their lumbering massiveness real, to make their lurching and jolting on this bumpy two-lane road real, but I don't have your language to transport these new, giant, tiny, swerving, lumbering, lurching, and jolting things.

I don't know the names.

I don't have your language to transport these giant, tiny, swerving, lumbering, lurching, and jolting things, because I couldn't learn your language.

I couldn't learn your language, Luddie, even though I tried and tried.

When I was a boy, I tried. As I brushed my teeth in the green guest bathroom of the Bombardier's home, I tried.

It seemed easier then.

The Bombardier brushed his teeth with me in the green guest bathroom, and he taught me some of your language as we brushed.

We brushed our teeth side by side in the big mirror in the green guest bathroom, me in my blue, footed pajamas, he in his blue cotton pajama top and bottom.

"Do you know what you want for your birthday?" he asked in English.

I spat in the sink and bared my clean teeth at the mirror.

"Nope," I said in English and wiped my lips.

"Nie," he said and thrust his brush around his molars.

"What?" I asked in English.

I held my blue toothbrush in my hand.

I stood on a little stool.

"'Nie,'" he said and spat, "is how you say 'no' in Polish."

"Nie," I said, watching my mouth in the mirror.

The bottom lip came down, then the tongue flopped forward and fell.

"'Tak,'" he said, running the water to rinse the bowl, "is how you say 'yes.'"

"Tak," I said to the mirror.

My jaw sprang down and froze.

"Are you ready for bed?" he asked in English.

My bottom lip came down, and my tongue flopped forward.

"Nie," I said.

"Oh you!" he said in English and scooped me up from the little stool to take me to bed.

My bottom lip came down, and my tongue flopped forward again and again and again, and I screamed with laughter.

Dear Luddie,

I thought I had learned a new language there in the bathroom, so when I was in high school, when I was less of a boy and more of a man, but barely, I tried to learn more of your language, because I thought it would be as easy as "tak" and "nie."

"Dzień dobry," the Bombardier would say to me when I was in high school.

"Dzień dobry," I would say back.

We would smile at each other in our new language, but secretly I wasn't so sure about this language, Luddie.

It had become much harder than just "tak" and "nie."

Every morning I would sit in my Polish classroom with my hat pulled low over my oily, bursting face, and I would listen to the teacher give me words in your language.

"Dzień dobry," she would say slowly, pointing her piece of chalk at the three of us who were trying to learn Polish.

"Dziękuję," she wrote on the green chalkboard.

"Tak," we said.

Words in your language floated up on the green chalkboard, and I copied them down in my notebook, but they never stayed.

The page would tear out, or I would draw pictures of skulls and brains all over the words.

Ms. Rothstein tried to put these words in a system for us, a system of worksheets and scenes, books and tapes, but this system didn't help keep the words in my head.

The words kept floating out, passing over my brain and slipping past my skull, so I tried to develop my own system.

I tried to understand your language with my own system of metaphors from my language.

I tried to understand.

My tapes and my books and my system tried to give me words and sounds from your language to make a new kind of world real, but when I tried to put these words and sounds into my system of metaphors from my language, I became a weird, wordless creature.

I became weird and wordless, and it was dangerous and terrifying because I couldn't understand anything.

I couldn't understand anything, but because I was a boy turning into a man I thought danger and terror would go away if I made their cause into a silly adventure, like building a tower with blocks.

I thought learning a new language could be like building a tower with blocks, or like a silly adventure a boy might have with a girl, so I made my system of metaphors and tried to learn from it.

"If I think of English words that resemble the sounds of the Polish words," I thought then, with my hat pulled low over my oily, bursting face, "I can make a story using these English words that sound like the Polish words. This story I make will help me remember the meaning of the Polish words, and before long I will know a new language."

It was like a cartoon. A bubble appeared above my head. A lightbulb. A system.

It seemed like a good thing, so I was a good boy and tried to build this tower through silly adventure.

I sat in the cold classroom in the morning, and I thought, "dzień dobry" is "good day" in Polish, which is what a good boy would say when meeting someone unfamiliar in Poland.

I didn't like gin, so I was unfamiliar with it, and I was also unfamiliar with anyone named Dobie, so, in my silly adventure system of easy metaphors, if I would meet Dobie in a bar drinking gin in Poland, I would say, "Dzień dobry" like a good boy.

Haha, I thought, good. I am learning Polish like June Tulle learned to be a woman by giving blowjobs on the back of the bus.

"Cześć," I went on with my system, is "hello" in Polish, which is what a good boy would say when meeting someone familiar.

If a good boy meets June Tulle and she is naked, I thought, the good boy is probably familiar with June Tulle. If this good boy is familiar with this naked June Tulle, he can probably touch her chest.

In my system, a good boy sees June Tulle naked in Poland, touches her chest, and says, "Cześć, cześć."

The system, I hope, is becoming clear, Luddie.

"Dziękuję" is "thank you" in Polish, which is what a good boy would say if someone did something nice.

If a good boy were in Poland and he went to Auschwitz and at Auschwitz the person beside him kept cooing and saying "yay," a good boy would wish for that person to be shanked.

If someone stuck a shank in a person cooing and saying "yay" at Auschwitz, a good boy would say "Dziękuję" to this someone.

It would be a silly adventure.

"Do widzenia" is "good-bye," which is what a good boy would say when leaving a person or place in Poland.

If a good boy leaves a person or a place in Poland because he must go feed dough to Zen ya-yas, a good boy would be leaving to dough-feed Zen ya-yas.

As a good boy left to do this in Poland, he would say, "Do widzenia." Haha.

"Jestem Amerykaninem" is "I am an American," which is what a good boy would say to someone to introduce his nationality. If a good boy were talking to a plant somewhere in Poland, this plant might want to talk about the United States. If this plant did want to talk about the

United States, a good boy might have to agree that the United States is crude and brutal.

"Yes, stem," a good boy would say, "America knees 'em."

"Jestem Amerykaninem."

Good boy.

"Nie rozumiem" is "I don't understand," which is what you would say if you were confused in Poland.

If a good boy happened to see a girl named Nia Rose, whom he went to elementary school with, a good boy would be confused.

If Nia Rose were a superhero with a special power called Zoomy, and she were flanked by adversaries in Poland, a good boy would be confused but he would want to say some kind of encouragement, so a good boy would yell, "Nia Rose! Zoomy 'em!" which she could do and then a good boy could go clear up his confusion over sodas with Nia in your country.

"Nie rozumiem."

This system worked for a short time when I tried to learn your language from more than just books and tapes.

This system worked for a short time when I would raise my hand every morning and answer the teacher's questions in Polish, but soon I became very confused.

Soon I became very confused, like when June Tulle the blowjob queen gave me a love note in social studies class.

"You're cute," it said. "What bus do you take?"

I became very confused because I had created a world of old stories out of the new language, and soon these stories strayed from the lessons I had hoped they could teach. The new language strayed from the lessons I intended, and so the new language turned on me.

The new language distorted my metaphors, changed my memories, my ideas, and my stories.

The new language jolted and terrified me and tried to make me into an insane babbling subhuman creature getting blowjobs in the back of a bus.

I was an adolescent without words for my bubbling brain, so my tower tumbled through the trees.

In my bubbling brain, Nia Rose looked at me savagely when I yelled "Zoomy 'em," because she never forgave me for saying I wanted to be like Martin Luther King, Jr. in seventh grade.

In seventh grade, she was my girlfriend, but she knew I would never be like Martin Luther King, Jr., so she dumped me.

I would never be like Martin Luther King, Jr. because I didn't love Nia Rose, I only loved the way she smelled and her friends.

I loved the way she smelled because she smelled like dough. She smelled like the dough I could feed to a Zen ya-ya.

I could feed Nia's doughy smell to the Zen ya-yas and also to the plant stem.

I could feed Nia's doughy smell to the plant stem so it could grow in fast motion as I spoke to it about the United States. It could grow in fast motion into a palm tree in a future city prospering with fast food chains, airports, and statues of American presidents. In this future city no one would knee anyone else, so I would go drink gin at a hotel bar and talk about the old days of kneeing 'em with Dobie. Dobie and I would become great friends as we would talk about the old days of kneeing 'em, so he would take me up to his room where many familiar Polish women would offer their chests for me to feel, but I wouldn't understand what to do because I wouldn't know their language.

Dear Luddie,

Before we left Chicago I asked the Bombardier in my old familiar language how he studied Polish.

He knew I had failed completely in high school trying to learn your language, so he knew he was the authority on your language now.

"When I studied Polish," the Bombardier said, "is quite a story."

He patted me on the back and picked some lint off of his trousers.

"When I studied Polish," he said, "I was seated across from an old Slavic languages professor in a dark wood-paneled room filled with old books. This was at the University, where I studied on the G.I. Bill.

"The old Slavic languages professor was from the Ukraine, and he came over to the United States between the wars.

"This old Slavic languages professor from the Ukraine leaned close and asked me, in Polish, what I studied as a major.

"His breath had the faintest pinch of garlic.

"In Polish, I said, 'I am studying political science.'

"The old Slavic languages professor asked me, in Polish, where I was from.

"In Polish, I said, 'I'm from here. The Midwest.'

"The old Slavic languages professor asked me, in Polish, what I did in the war.

"In Polish, I said, 'I dropped bombs on the Nazis.'

"Then, out of turn, I asked in English, 'When will I take the test?'

"The old Slavic languages professor answered, in Polish, 'You just did.'"

Dear Luddie,

I will try to tell you the story of what happens to us with what I have.

Your language turned me into a weird wordless creature when I was in high school, so I won't be able to make the giant lurching trucks and the tiny swerving cars real for you in these letters.

I'm sorry.

I won't be able to make the giant lurching trucks and the tiny swerving cars real, I'll only be able to make what I have real.

What I have is giant, tiny, lurching, and swerving.

What I have is "samochódy."

What I have is "dzień dobry."

What I have is "Dziękuję."

What I have is "tak."

What I have is "nostrovia."

I will try to build a tower of these words and the words in my language. They are what I have.

I will try to put you in this tower so you can see out all across history from this tower, from your spot in the wild blue yonder, and hopefully you will see us clearly somewhere in your country.

I won't giggle.

I will simply tell you what happens to us with my language.

I will try to be a good correspondent.

Dear Luddie,

Wroclaw is where we begin.

Here in Wroclaw, we bring our luggage into a five-hundred-year-old hotel, and in the five-hundred-year-old hotel we sign a form on a plastic countertop and lean against the badly upholstered chairs.

We get two rooms at the five-hundred-year-old hotel with plastic countertops and bad upholstery, and we drag our luggage up the stairs to these rooms.

Bernadette and I stumble into our room, and the Bombardier stumbles into his.

"Good night to you both," the Bombardier says. "Tomorrow we will look for Blechhammer on the Oder bright and early!"

Blechhammer, the bombed synthetic oil factory on the Oder River.

"Good night," we say, "bright and early, Blechhammer on the Oder!"

We shut our door wearily.

We shut our door wearily because it's late, and we are all scraped out from our first adventure in Poland with the Bombardier.

We sigh.

It's been a full day of driving.

We sigh and look around the room we have stumbled into after our full day of driving.

It is a mess of five-hundred-year-old things and twenty-year-old things.

We look around.

The creaky, wide-board wooden floor is five hundred years old with deep cracks and fissures, but it has twenty-year-old black paint covering it.

A draft chills our feet.

The framed paintings of chartreuse sailboats on the walls are twenty years old, but the crumbling walls they hang on are five hundred years old.

The deeply weathered ceiling of the room we stumble into, five hundred years old, the fire-retardant curtains, twenty.

The console TV, the window frames.

The molding, the light fixtures.

The mess of the room we have stumbled into is marvelous and strange, and it reaches outside the room into the city itself.

The marvelous and strange mess stretches out into the city outside our twenty-year-old curtains, out into the flying buttresses of a five-hundred-year-old church.

This is Wroclaw, Poland.

"This is Wroclaw, Poland," I say to Bernadette as she steps into the twenty-year-old shower, "suspended in both the process of decay and the process of masking decay."

"What?" she yells from the shower.

"Nothing," I say from the bed, not smart.

I lie down on the bed in Wroclaw, Poland, in the process of decay, and through the twenty-year-old shower curtain, I can see the outline of Bernadette showering.

The bed is not really one bed, but two beds shoved together.

"Are you okay?" I ask as Bernadette plops onto the two beds after her shower.

"Yes," she says with a sigh, "just covered in car feeling."

We rest in silence on top of the twenty-year-old bedspreads, covered in car feeling, listening to the drunks of Wroclaw laugh and yell on the five-hundred-year-old cobblestone street below our window.

"Did I ever tell you," Bernadette asks, "that when I was a girl I used to fantasize God would make me pregnant?"

"Nope," I say.

Her voice is calm and light, a little dreamy.

"I used to lie awake at night," Bernadette says, "terrified God would send his baby into my belly."

"I've always thought you were a good sleeper," I say.

"I am," Bernadette says, "but I used to lie awake at night, not sleeping, praying to God not to send his baby into my belly, not to make me wake up in the morning pregnant with his baby."

"This is a fantasy?" I say, pressing my palm onto the twenty-year-old bedspread. "I don't have these kinds of fantasies."

"I told my Mom that God terrified me," Bernadette says, "but my Mom said I didn't understand the story of Mary. She says, in that story, the baby is the important thing, not Mary."

"This must be some kind of girl fantasy," I say.

"In that story," Bernadette says, "no one ever thinks about Mary waking up one morning with God's baby in her belly. It's terrifying, to wake up with a baby in your belly. I don't want to have God's baby in my belly. I don't want God to be the daddy."

She turns over in her towel to face me.

"I want to be the daddy," she says, facing me. Her eyes are brown but not like a normal brown, more like a magic gypsy brown. The kind of eyes people say you get lost in, fall in love with, die for.

"You don't want God to be the daddy?" I say.

"I want to be the daddy," Bernadette says, "so I pray to God not to put his baby in my belly."

"You still pray to God and ask him this?" I ask.

"I still pray to God," Bernadette says.

"And God still hasn't put his baby in your belly?" I ask.

"No, he still hasn't," Bernadette says, patting her belly.

"So your prayers have been answered!" I say.

"Yep," Bernadette says.

"Your prayers have been answered," I say, "but you'll still never be a daddy."

Her slightly sideways smile smiles, and her dark brown eyes flash.

"You can fantasize you're the daddy if you want to," I say, pulling her across the bed divide, "because you want to be the daddy so much, and I don't want to be the daddy at all!"

We laugh.

I say this, and we laugh, and Bernadette kisses me across the divide and then, because no one will be the daddy, we practice making a baby.

We practice making a baby in our five-hundred-year-old hotel while the drunks of Wroclaw walk beside the church, and the Bombardier sleeps in his room, and God stays in no one's belly.

I hear the drunks laughing and yelling outside the church as Bernadette and I practice making a baby, and I wonder if anyone should ever want to be a daddy in Poland.

Bernadette, without pretending, practices making a baby with me, and she is beautiful and small and in my hands, which are not the hands of a daddy or a god.

Then, after we practice making our baby, Bernadette falls asleep like a good sleeper, but I do not.

I don't fall asleep because I hear the drunks, and I wonder if Bernadette has taken her birth control pill, and I wonder, if she hasn't taken her birth control pill, if I didn't just become a daddy in Poland.

I wonder if I didn't just become a daddy in Poland, and I listen to the drunks of Wroclaw laughing and yelling outside the church.

For a moment, there's a baby in Bernadette's belly, and it has a beard like Jesus, but then it doesn't. It's just a little orange baby in a belly, I think.

I wonder, if Bernadette hasn't taken her birth control pill, what will happen to this baby we have just made in Wroclaw, Poland?

I close my eyes and see a small Polish baby, just made, floating in Bernadette's sleeping belly.

I hear loud, Polish yelling.

I see Polish drunkards and pee-spattered churches.

I feel fast-moving little junk cars speeding around me.

I see a small Polish baby, and I hear loud Polish yelling, and I see pee-spattered churches, and I feel fast-moving little junk cars, so I roll over and try not to think of Polish babies and yelling and pee and cars and daddies, and I try to sleep in my bed.

I try to sleep in my bed, but I can't sleep because I can't stop thinking about Polish babies.

Some Polish babies, I think in my bed, grow up to become Polish women.

Polish women. They haunt me just a little. When I got drunk at a Christmas party last year, my brother told me I should think about Polish women.

"What do you know about Poland?" my brother asked me at this Christmas party.

"Not much," I said, already drunk, "besides the Bombardier's story."

"Forget the Bombardier's story," he says. "What do you know about Polish women?"

"I guess," I said, "nothing?"

"Nothing," he said. "Not even what they look like?"

"Nothing," I said, "but I would guess they are tough and cool, with five-hundred-year-old eyes. Spiky hair. Tight black jeans."

"You can't ever know a country," he said, shaking his closely shaved fat red head, "without knowing the women."

"Hmm," I said, drinking more beer.

"Women," he told me in a low voice, "can be known on the Internet.

"On the Internet," he told me in this low voice, "there are lots of Polish women you can get to know."

In this low voice, he told me where I could get to know Polish women on the Internet, so when Bernadette and I got home from this Christmas party she went to bed, and I went to the computer.

We did not practice making babies that night.

We did not practice making babies that night because Bernadette went to bed, and I went to the computer to look for Polish women on the Internet like my brother told me to.

Looking for Polish women on the Internet I found a web site filled with women I could get to know.

I could get to know women from many different countries on this web site.

I could get to know many different countries through many different women on this web site, but I couldn't get to know anyone's real name because on this web site, no one used their real names.

On this web site, everyone had a new name like "44DCOED" or "BigDaddysGirl."

44DCOED and BigDaddysGirl had new names and webcams on this web site filled with women.

On this web site, with these webcams, with these new names, these women, 44DCOED and BigDaddysGirl, waited to talk with me.

44DCOED and BigDaddysGirl waited to talk with me, and if I wanted, I could pay 44DCOED and BigDaddysGirl to not only talk with me but to take their clothes off for me and pretend to make a baby with me.

On this web site filled with women from different countries, I searched and searched for the right Polish woman to get to know, someone tough and cool, with tight black jeans, living in a blocky apartment building, but it took a long time.

Finally, after saying no to 44DCOED after 44DCOED, I found the right Polish woman to get to know.

The one I found was young and slim with short spiky pink hair.

Her name was PolishBaby4U and I agreed to pay $1.99 a minute to talk with her, to see her take her clothes off, to pretend to make a baby with her.

I agreed to pay $1.99 a minute to get to know her.

A video screen popped up on my computer with a flashing cursor beside it.

This young Polish woman with short spiky pink hair sat in her lacy underwear looking at her webcam.

The flashing cursor beside her said "Hey" in red letters.

I read the letters and looked at PolishBaby4U on the screen, but I didn't know how to get to know her.

Should I ask if she knows you? I wondered.

Should I say I would like to see her take off her clothes?

Should I say I want to pretend to make a baby with her?

PolishBaby4U stroked her chest and made eyes at me.

I watched her stroke her chest and make eyes at me, and I decided typing red letters to PolishBaby4U would not be so different than talking with PolishBaby4U in real life, so I typed in red letters what I would have said to PolishBaby4U in real life.

"Where are you from?" I typed.

PolishBaby4U smiled into her webcam and rubbed her breasts a little more before leaning over to type.

"I am in Poland," she typed in red letters.

I typed back.

"Where in Poland?"

She typed back.

"In Wroclaw."

As I read what she typed in red letters, I thought of how I truly knew nothing about Poland.

Where is Wroclaw? I wondered.

Do lots of young Polish women in Wroclaw have webcams?

What time is it in Wroclaw?

Do lots of young Polish women in Wroclaw, I wondered, know about Blechhammer?

In red letters I typed, "The Bombardier was shot down in Poland. He was sheltered from the Nazis by Luddie during World War II."

PolishBaby4U had begun making more serious eyes at me and rubbing her lacy black hips.

She smiled a little and leaned in to type.

Her breasts swung down toward the keyboard.

"Yes," she typed. "There are many stories like this in Poland. My family had it hard during the war. Many died."

I sat looking at these red letters on the screen.

PolishBaby4U sat looking at her webcam.

She no longer made eyes.

She just looked.

What had I gotten to know?

Dear Luddie,

The brightness comes early in Wroclaw.

The brightness comes early, and the Bombardier comes with it, knocking on our door in this five-hundred-year-old hotel.

The Bombardier knocks on our door and says, "Rise and shine" because he wants to go to the Wroclaw Gazette.

Bright and early in the morning he wants to go to the Wroclaw Gazette so he can ask an expert about the Blechhammer oil factory he bombed sixty years ago in your country.

Bright and early, without breakfast, Bernadette, the Bombardier, and I walk from the five-hundred-year-old hotel into the pedestrian mall of Wroclaw with its pastel storefronts and cobblestone streets.

The light is sharp.

Bright and early, dressed in our winter clothes, we walk past the gothic Wroclaw City Hall that, even bright and early in the morning, has house music pumping out from the basement.

"Weird," Bernadette says, and I nod.

"Weird Wroclaw," she says.

"Breslau," I say, "to the Germans."

We stop in our winter clothes at a small pastel shop beside the house music city hall for breakfast.

Bright and early, the small pastel shop beside the city hall has no breakfast, only tea and coffee.

I feel tired, whiny, and reckless in the pastel shop beside the city hall, because I got no sleep last night, thinking too much about Polish women.

I got no sleep because I thought too much about Polish women, so I order a Polish breakfast tea.

Tired, whiny, and reckless because I got no sleep, I order the Polish breakfast tea Herbata z rumem and drink it down in a few reckless gulps while Bernadette and the Bombardier sip their coffee.

I order another.

"Bring it on," I say.

"What is Herbata z rumem?" Bernadette asks.

"No idea," I say and smack my lips.

After I drink the next Herbata z rumem in a few reckless gulps and smack my lips and Bernadette and the Bombardier sip their coffee, we walk down the cobblestone streets in our winter clothes to the Gazette office.

The Bombardier wears his brown leather bomber jacket and his brown hat with a feather in it.

I wear my black wool winter coat and an orange hunting cap.

Bernadette wears her pink winter coat and earmuffs.

We are three American tourists in your country, Luddie.

It is springtime, but we're cold.

In the Gazette office, in his brown leather bomber jacket, in Polish, the Bombardier asks the young woman at the reception desk if the paper has any World War II experts.

The young woman at the reception desk, a blonde in kneesocks and a cardigan sweater, smiles a beautiful smile and holds up a slim finger, politely signaling for the Bombardier to wait while she finishes writing on a form.

The receptionist, I think, feeling the Herbata z rumem work in my empty stomach, is a Polish woman my brother might have gotten to know on the Internet.

I begin to feel ill.

After she finishes writing on a form, the receptionist speaks rapidly in Polish to the Bombardier, but the Bombardier does not understand this rapidly spoken Polish, so he chuckles and shrugs.

The receptionist smiles her beautiful smile again and says in clear English, "With whom would you like to speak?"

"Do you have any experts here," the Bombardier asks in clear English, "who could help me find the Blechhammer oil factory?"

The receptionist listens to the Bombardier, and then she nods.

"Sixty years ago I bombed it," he says.

She nods and then she picks up a phone and speaks rapidly into it in Polish.

"An expert will be down shortly," she says to us in English.

Bernadette and the Bombardier adjust their winter clothes and I watch the receptionist scratch her long kneesocked leg.

Shortly, an expert comes down the stairs to greet us.

This young woman who comes down the stairs to greet us has pink hair molded into spiky clumps.

She wears a latex miniskirt.

This young woman with pink, spiky hair and a latex miniskirt shakes our hands and speaks very clear English, but she is not the kind of expert we need.

"There are many stories like this in Poland," she says. "I'm sorry."

She sips water out of a blue plastic bottle she has clipped to her backpack.

"Is there anything else I can help you with?" she asks in clear English.

The Bombardier thinks and then looks over to me.

The Bombardier looks over to me, but I can only slowly shake my head no because I am feeling very ill.

I am feeling very ill because Herbata z rumem is black tea with a shot of cheap rum in it. I've figured it out—"herbata," tea; "rumem," rum— but I didn't need to know your language to know, Luddie.

I can tell by my burps.

Herbata z rumem is black tea with a shot of cheap rum in it, and the expert has short spiky pink hair, so I slowly shake my head no.

What does my brother know about Poland, I wonder, burping, that I don't?

Dejected, the Bombardier leads us back down the cobblestone streets to the five-hundred-year-old hotel, where he says, "I'll meet you two down at the car in fifteen minutes, and then we'll go find Blechhammer."

The Bombardier slaps me on the back and marches into his room.

I stumble into our room and fall into the bathroom where I throw up, because I have a stomach full of Herbata z rumem and nothing else.

I have a delicate system, Luddie.

I have a stomach full of Herbata z rumem and nothing else, and the expert looked tough and cool with short spiky pink hair, so I throw up in the bathroom.

I say to Bernadette, who stands behind me in her pink vinyl coat, "I can't drive to Blechhammer like this."

"Your puke smells like rum," Bernadette says.

I retch again.

Bernadette rubs the back of my black wool winter coat gently.

"She's not one of the girls from the Internet," she says.

I sputter into the bowl.

"What girls?"

"Funny," Bernadette says, then she gives my back a hard slap. She goes down to the hotel restaurant.

There, she orders a big breakfast tray with rolls, sausage, hard-boiled eggs, fruit, and more black tea and more meat. Lots of meat, which we've hardly eaten in years. While she goes down to the hotel restaurant, I lay in the bathroom counting to ten.

Should I have gotten to know this country more before we came? I wonder.

Should I have learned about Herbata z rumem and women?

Just as I count to ten for the last time before the Herbata z rumem turns my delicate system completely out, Bernadette arrives with the big breakfast tray.

Bernadette arrives with the big breakfast tray and feeds me a little roll, and a little fruit.

"You need to eat some meat," she says, "and toughen up."

After Bernadette feeds me a little roll and a little fruit, I eat the sausage and hard-boiled eggs. I eat the ham and the bacon and the blood and the tissue and the fat. I eat the meat. I toughen up.

I eat the meat and the Bombardier packs his things in his room down the hall.

Bernadette eats a roll.

I eat the sausage and eggs, the Bombardier packs his things, Bernadette eats a roll, and young Polish women rub their breasts on the Internet.

They rub their breasts on the Internet and think about their dead families and my brother watches them, getting to know this country while I eat meat to keep from puking rum and toughen up.

7

Dear Luddie,

Let me back up a little. Let me tell you a story.

In late December, after the Bombardier burned a dishtowel and after I said yes, the Bombardier and I began to plan our adventure in your country.

In late December, as we planned our adventure in your country, the Bombardier and I began to talk about maps.

"Should I get a road map?" I asked.

"No," the Bombardier said.

"We'll get a road map samochódy once we get in to Polska?" I asked.

"Tak," he said.

I sat on an old couch in the den of the Bombardier's retirement condo, and the Bombardier sat adjacent to me on a folding chair.

He had his hands clasped on his lap, and he smiled at me as I said "samochódy" and "Polska."

The weather had been mild in the Midwest over Christmas and I only wore a light sweater.

The Bombardier wore a Western-style shirt and sky blue Wrangler jeans.

The map talk had caused him to withdraw into his thoughts for a moment, but he emerged from these thoughts buoyant.

He gave a little clap and looked up at me with a big smile.

"I've showed you my escape map haven't I?" he said.

I shook my head, "No."

He hopped over to his metal desk, opening drawers and rummaging through plastic bags that had been stuffed behind rows and rows of small spiral-bound notepads.

"Doggone it," he said and shoved a row of notepads into the back of the drawer.

"Doggone it," he said again and pulled a small leather satchel out from the drawer.

In this small leather satchel were what looked to me like pale, mustard-colored handkerchiefs. They were nylon escape maps from two wars.

"The military gave these maps to each airman," the Bombardier said, "along with a first aid kit and some food, just in case his plane got shot down."

The Bombardier roughly spread each map out on his lap as if they were one-and-a-half-square-foot slabs of dough.

"No. This is Norway, and this one," he said, holding the second cloth up in front of his face, "is from Korea."

He wadded both maps back up and stuffed them into the satchel, then went back to the desk.

As he rummaged through his desk again, I pulled the wadded-up Norway map out of the satchel and ran my hand over it.

It felt like an old nightgown.

"All right," he said, standing up from the desk, "here it is."

He held up his map from your country, Luddie. It had been no more lovingly cared for than the others—it had been wadded and stuffed—but the Bombardier now held this map slightly more reverently because, I thought then, he had actually used it once and might again in a few months when we would begin our adventure in your country.

I saw the words Breslau, Blechhammer, Oder, Gleiwitz, Rzeszów, Praha, and Frankfurt on the map.

Breslau, Blechhammer, Oder, Gleiwitz, Rzeszów, Praha, and Frankfurt were all marked with a thick grease pencil.

These heavy marks were zs for flack and widening circles around the bombing targets.

A long black line ran across the center of the map—starting in Russia, traveling over Hindenburg and Gleiwitz, and ending at two red squares marked Blechhammer North and Blechhammer South on the Oder River.

Dear Luddie,

Bernadette, the Bombardier, and I drive along the highway beside the Oder River in your country toward Blechhammer North and Blechhammer South.

We drive toward what we think might be these Blechhammers, but we don't know for sure because these Blechhammers are not on our road map samochódy.

The Blechhammers are not on our atlas.

The Blechhammers are not on the road map samochódy or on our atlas, but they are on the Bombardier's escape map.

The Blechhammers are on the Bombardier's escape map, but the Bombardier's escape map confuses us because the names on the escape map are all in German, and the names on the roads in front of us are all in Polish.

The old nylon escape map confuses us because the grease pencil has smudged and obscured the German names.

What is Wroclaw on the road is Breslau on the escape map.

What is Brzeg on the road is Brieg on the escape map.

What is a bend in the Oder River is a black smudge on the escape map.

The road and the escape map do not correspond clearly, so we put the escape map away, and we look at the road map samochódy and the atlas, but they don't tell us about the Blechhammers, so we ask the Bombardier where we should go.

The Bombardier thinks for a minute, looking at the road map and then out into the straw and dirt, and then he says we should go to Brzeg because he remembers opening the bomb-bay doors near Brzeg, over Opole.

He remembers opening the bomb-bay doors over Opole, and he remembers dropping the bombs near Brzeg.

"I remember the initial point was near Opole," he says from the backseat of the samochódy, "the I.P., and we were heading northwest, so Brzeg has got to be the place."

We drive down the road, heading southeast under the bright morning sky, following the Bombardier's memory.

Dear Luddie,

Under the bright morning sky, after about an hour on the full four-lane expressway leading from Wroclaw to Krakow, we pull off onto another bumpy two-lane highway that leads the ten miles north to Brzeg.

For ten miles, we watch small piles of snow melt on the edges of this bumpy two-lane highway.

It is a warm spring in your country, Luddie.

Everyone has said so.

Even though it is a warm spring, we still have the heat on in our samochódy, but we're starting to feel more at home in this warm spring in your country. I stretch my arm out and yell, "First one in Brzeg!"

Brzeg is a little Polish town on a bumpy two-lane highway surrounded by small piles of snow melting in this warm spring.

We've already seen quite a few little Polish towns as we've driven through your country, so we know that in little Polish towns there are always little Polish strip malls squatting in between the bumpy two-lane highways and the snowy farmland.

These squatting strip malls in little Polish towns are block-long, one-story stretches of storefronts with small sidewalks and lines of parking spaces jutting out onto the road.

These squatting strip malls are useful, we've seen, but these squatting strip malls are also very very ugly.

We pull into a jutting parking space in the useful but ugly squatting strip mall of Brzeg, and as soon as I turn off the engine, the Bombardier bolts out onto the sidewalk.

The Bombardier bolts out on to the sidewalk and asks a woman in a soiled parka if she knows Blechhammer.

The woman shakes her head and puts out her hand.

The Bombardier looks down at her hand and then asks her again more slowly about Blechhammer.

The woman in the soiled parka puts out her hand again more forcefully.

The Bombardier asks again, loudly and slowly, but the woman in the soiled parka finally shakes her head and walks on down the sidewalk under the bright morning sky of Brzeg.

She wants money, and the Bombardier wants information, but neither understands the other, so they walk away.

Undaunted, the Bombardier waves Bernadette and me over.

Under the bright morning sky of Brzeg, we follow him down the sidewalk of the squatting Polish strip mall. In his slightly stooped manner, the Bombardier walks up to more passersby in this squatting Polish strip mall, but all the passersby shrug their shoulders or shake their heads.

No one understands.

No one recognizes the name Blechhammer.

No one understands or recognizes the name, because no one has lived long enough to understand or recognize the name, and when I think of this, for the first time in my life, the sentence, "The Bombardier is old," floats into my mind.

The sentence floats into my mind written on a sheet of yellowing paper, in black ink.

"The Bombardier is old."

Because the Bombardier looks at me clearly, jokes with me, and walks freely here in your country, I have never thought of this sentence before. I've never thought of how many years eighty-four really is.

Eighty-four years is a long time, Luddie.

Eighty-four years is one long lifetime of eating, drinking, sleeping, and walking.

Eighty-four years is enough to grind a body down to almost nothing.

Eighty-four years is enough to unstring a mind.

Eighty-four years is enough to kill a person, but the eighty-four-year-old Bombardier walks briskly up to a man sitting on a milk crate on the sidewalk here in Brzeg as if it were the first day of his adult life.

A stench of alcohol surrounds this man on the milk crate.

A stench not just of alcohol but alcohol seeping through pores surrounds this man on the milk crate.

This man on the milk crate looks to have lived long enough to understand, but he also looks to have lived long enough to be ground down and unstrung.

He has no teeth.

He has a craggy, drooping face.

He has ropy, gnarled hands.

He smells like alcohol and pores.

He has all of these signs of old age, but when the Bombardier asks this no-teeth, craggy, drooping-faced man on a milk crate about Blechhammer and the war, the man says in bitter broken English, "I have fifty-six! No war with you!"

Alcohol and pores waft over us.

I watch Bernadette gag.

I feel the stirrings of Herbata z rumem and meat in my stomach.

My delicate system.

The Bombardier walks off, waving his hand in front of his face.

"Fifty-six!" he whispers to me as we walk.

Fifty-six and no teeth. Fifty-six and a craggy, drooping face. Fifty-six and ropy, gnarled hands.

As we walk away from this man, I watch the Bombardier and think, eighty-four and a wool suit. Eighty-four and a feathered hat. Eighty-four and a brisk walk.

I watch the Bombardier and feel a surge of dread.

"The Bombardier is old."

Dear Luddie,

From what we have seen so far in your country, the no-teeth, craggy, drooping face has been the face of the men in your country.

The alcohol and pores smell has been the smell of the men in your country.

I don't mean any offense, but we have seen no men older than fifty-six in your country without craggy, drooping faces.

We have seen no men without the alcohol and pores smell.

What has happened to all of your men, Luddie?

Why are their faces and their smells so wrong?

Everyone younger than fifty-six, everyone with a normal face and normal smell, has been a woman.

All of these younger-than fifty-six women have had teeth and very smooth, taut faces, and light perfumy smells, but these women don't understand the Bombardier's story.

They don't understand an American man returning to the town where he dropped bombs sixty years before.

Who will understand, Luddie, if not the women or the men with their faces and smells?

We don't know who will understand, but we have reason to believe someone will understand because we have read books.

We have read books and in these books people understand, so we go where we think we might be understood—a bookshop.

Surely, we think, a bookshop will understand. A bookshop will expand the time of this country and let a little understanding in, we think, so we step into a small bookshop in this squatting strip mall of Brzeg, hoping to find someone who has expanded time enough to understand, with or without a wrong face or smell.

The Bombardier walks to the counter of the bookshop, up to a man with a saggy face, and I walk to the history books.

In the history books, I see men old enough to understand the Bombardier's story on the covers.

These men stand stately in their uniforms, in graying and yellowing photographs, with swords and guns, but after I pick these books up, I see it is not the men themselves putting their own pictures on these book covers.

I turn the books over, or open their flaps, and I see young, smooth faces smiling idiot smiles out at me.

I see these young, smooth smiling faces, and I see it is not the stately men with swords and guns who put these pictures on the book covers, but the survivors of these men.

It is the survivors of these men with swords and guns who want to tell the stories of these men with swords and guns, I think, touching the glossy nose of a man with a sword on a book cover.

These young, smooth smiling faces want to tell these stories to make some sense of what remains in this time in this country.

I see these smiling faces are as wrong as the drooping ones. They won't understand. I look up from the glossy nose on the book cover at the sound of the Bombardier's voice.

"No one here has heard of Blechhammer," he says with a confused smile.

Dear Luddie,

Lagging behind the striding Bombardier, I look at Bernadette, asking her with my eyes if we should do something more to help the Bombardier and his story.

Bernadette turns her palms up and shrugs. There isn't anything we can do to help the Bombardier and his story now.

There isn't anything we can do because the Bombardier is striding into a pharmacy around the corner with us or without us.

The Bombardier is striding into the pharmacy with us or without us, still moving quickly and assuredly.

By the time Bernadette and I walk in the door of the pharmacy, the Bombardier has already started his story for the smooth-faced, toothy young woman behind the glass partition.

The smooth-faced, toothy young woman behind the glass partition has dark brown hair, a lab coat, and cat's-eye glasses.

She smells nice, but she can't understand.

She answers the Bombardier in Polish, and he leans in to hear her better, banging his head on the glass partition.

I watch his brown hat with its feather fall to the floor after banging on the glass partition, and I wonder about the Bombardier's ears.

The Bombardier's ears are big, floppy, and pink, and they are eighty-four years old.

His big, floppy, eighty-four-year-old pink ears jut out from under his hat when his hat isn't falling to the floor, but his big, floppy, eighty-four-year-old pink jutting ears don't catch sounds very well.

They don't catch sounds very well, and so the Bombardier has fat plastic hearing aids stuck in his eighty-four-year-old ears to help him catch the sounds of people speaking.

For as long as I can remember, everyone has had to exaggerate the sounds of their speaking—to stretch their lips and to project their voices—for the Bombardier to catch and understand them, but everyone for as long as I can remember has indulged the Bombardier.

Everyone has indulged him for as long as I can remember—exaggerating their speech and stretching their lips—except the Bombardier's wife.

The Bombardier's wife didn't indulge him, Luddie.

Dear Luddie,

Let me tell you about the Bombardier's wife. I hate to bring her up, Luddie, but the Bombardier's wife was so beautiful and her story is important here. It's important because the Bombardier would never talk about Poland with her, about the war with her, or about you. He would never talk about these things with her but now that she is dead the Bombardier talks. He talks, but he does not talk about her.

The Bombardier's wife was from Chicago, and she loved company.

This is her story.

She and the Bombardier married after the war, after you, and after the war and you they had lots of company.

For forty years after the war and you, company came over with drinks and stories, and for forty years after the war and you, company loved the Bombardier's beautiful wife from Chicago who never indulged him.

For forty years after the war and you, the Bombardier's wife loved company, but she never indulged him, so when the Bombardier's hearing began to go, she would say, loudly, in front of company, "Why don't you put your damn hearing aids in?"

Company would always laugh.

The Bombardier wouldn't laugh, only cup his big floppy pink ear in his hand.

Company would always laugh even more then and company would continue to indulge him without his damn hearing aids in, exaggerating their speech and stretching their lips so he could understand.

The Bombardier's wife was no-nonsense. She was from Chicago, and she was beautiful, and company all knew it.

Then, one day, company began to whisper.

One day, company began to whisper because the Bombardier's wife had begun to be weird, but company didn't want the Bombardier to know how weird.

She began to waver in and out of conversation, veering into fantasy and reverie when company talked about City Hall or new parking meters, so company began to whisper, but the Bombardier couldn't hear them because his ears had already gotten old.

"I remember the men wouldn't leave the front lawn," she said to company, "until I had that baby."

Company listened and patted her on her blousy shoulder and then they began to whisper.

She laughed her brittle Chicago laugh and strode into the kitchen.

The Bombardier couldn't hear company whisper, so when he found his wife finally, lost in fantasy and reverie and unable to come back, he cried and cried.

"Imagine," she said to him dreamily, "a grown man crying in the company of a singer. Don't you have a mother?"

He cried and cried, but company didn't cry because they had known she was slowly going for years, so they indulged the devastated Bombardier, exaggerating their speech and stretching their lips around words of sympathy.

Company helped the devastated Bombardier find his wife a new home for the confused, after forty years and a life with the Bombardier, after she veered fully into fantasy and reverie, away from City Hall and parking meters, and company came to visit the Bombardier's wife in her confused home, even when she could no longer tell the difference between company and no company.

She had Alzheimer's, Luddie. Her memories slowly turned black in her brain.

"Ray Vaughn put talcum on the new roots," she said. "Ah yes. What a lovelorn tree that one was!"

Finally, after years of exaggerating and stretching words of sympathy, there was no company left except the Bombardier, who couldn't hear his wife's confused conversations, and in this unhearing but loving company the Bombardier's beautiful wife from Chicago died.

"Watch the morning," she said on her deathbed. "It's a tree."

The Bombardier watched her lips and nodded when she said this, and then he watched her die. She died and the Bombardier, in the middle of the exaggerated and stretched sympathy of her funeral said to me, "Don't *you* ever get old!"

The Bombardier's wife got old, Luddie, and she died, leaving the Bombardier with indulgent company who exaggerate and stretch their speech instead of telling him to put his damn hearing aids in.

That is a little of her story.

Dear Luddie,

Here in your country, no one indulges the Bombardier except me and Bernadette, but it's not the same.

It's not the same, so he has finally put his damn hearing aids in, but I'm afraid they aren't helping.

I'm afraid they aren't helping because I can see them in his big floppy pink ears, but I still have to exaggerate my speech and stretch my lips a little more for him to understand my sounds.

I'm afraid because I can see him trying to turn these hearing aids up after he bangs his head on the glass partition in this pharmacy, trying to hear the young woman with the cat's-eye glasses.

The Bombardier is eighty-four years old.

The young woman behind the glass partition finally, after a few more questions from the Bombardier, shakes her head resolutely, no.

She shakes her head no, but in one last effort, the Bombardier yells, "Synthetic. Oil. Factory." in loud, clear English.

The young woman doesn't understand, but an older woman farther behind the counter in a flowery smock hears the Bombardier yell "Synthetic. Oil. Factory." in loud, clear English and the older woman farther behind the counter in a flowery smock yelps, "Tak, tak!" and shuffles up to the counter.

The older woman in the flowery smock and the younger woman in cat's-eye glasses whisper in rapid Polish behind the counter and then the younger woman with dark brown hair, a lab coat, and cat's-eye glasses says, "Ahhh."

"Yes," the old woman yells in heavily accented English, "there is a *synthetic oil factory* in this town, but no one has ever called this *synthetic oil factory* 'Blechhammer' like you!"

The younger woman, who is probably in her late twenties, petite,

with her dark brown hair pulled back in a small bun, writes out directions on a prescription pad and then she smiles indulgently at the
Bombardier.

She yells through the glass partition, "This will get you!"

The Bombardier thanks her in Polish and then yells, in loud clear
English, "Do you have any prescription eye drops for glaucoma?"

The younger woman smiles again, but less indulgently.

"No!" she yells.

The Bombardier snaps his fingers and frowns.

"I know those eyehooks are cheap here," he whispers to Bernadette as
we walk out of the pharmacy.

Eyehooks.

Dear Luddie,

Sixty years ago, when the Bombardier's ears were fresh and in the war, the Bombardier's superiors barked orders into them. They barked orders to drop bombs from his Flying Fortress onto the Old World.

The Bombardier heard his superiors bark into his fresh ears clearly, so for three years he flew over the Old World in a Flying Fortress, dropping bombs on factories and towns.

He dropped bombs on Blechhammer.

Even though Blechhammer is just one of these factories in these towns, even though Blechhammer is just one of hundreds of places bombed in these three years of war, even though the Bombardier never saw Blechhammer except for the few minutes he sat above it in the Flying Fortress, Blechhammer is what he has come back to your country to see.

He has come back to your country to see Blechhammer, Luddie, even though it's only one point on a map full of points, because he wants to know what happened on the ground when he followed his orders in the air.

"I had been on nearly fifty bombing runs in the war," he says as we follow the young woman's directions to Blechhammer, "and by December of 1944 I was lead bombardier in a fleet of twenty-seven ships.

"On a bombing run, once the fleet reached the initial point," he says, "the fleet broke up into squadrons of nine ships, and these squadrons relied on the lead bombardier to guide them all to the target.

"In this case," he tells us, "I remember my fleet had broken off into squadrons at the I.P. over Opole where we came under heavy flack fire from the ground.

"And at that time we had already been hit by fighters, but these fighters fell off once we reached the I.P."

I try to picture the plane, the Bombardier's Flying Fortress, in the warm spring sky above us, but my mind fills with only a dull, grayish green color.

Sixty years ago the Bombardier's Flying Fortress had been hit by fighters, but he led the squadron here anyway.

The squadron dropped their bombs on this spot, despite the damage, because that's what their superiors told them to do.

Can you picture it, Luddie?

From the plane or from the ground?

"I don't know how many other squadrons suffered damage, but I assume quite a few," he says, "My plane went down just outside of Rzeszów, where the Russians had recently taken over."

Dear Luddie,

Over Christmas, I remember the Bombardier's radical daughter making tea in the kitchen of her house, talking about Blechhammer.

"I'm sure after such a traumatic experience—the war, yes, but being shot down in particular," she said to me, "the Bombardier would like to feel as if it were worth it."

The Bombardier's radical daughter poured steaming water into her cup and said, "You know, he wants to feel as if obeying orders, making it to Blechhammer, dropping the bombs, and keeping his cool played some kind of profound part in stopping all that evil."

She waved her hand in the air.

"He wants to know now," she said, "in the twilight of his life if what he did during his youth had any lasting effect.

"I just hope," she said, taking a sip, burning her lip a bit, "you're both not too disappointed by what you find."

"Right," I said.

How could we be disappointed by what we find, I thought, walking away from the kitchen of the radical daughter's house in disgust.

Now, turning a corner just outside of Brzeg, Bernadette, the Bombardier, and I see how we could be disappointed.

We see, rising above the tree line, what's left of Blechhammer.

Dear Luddie,

As we pull into the parking lot, we see four huge vats, dozens of yellow emissions towers, and a web of scaffolding all spread along the banks of the Oder River.

We see all of this reach up into the bright spring sky as if it had never been through a war, as if no bombs had ever been dropped on it.

We drive around to the back entrance and the Bombardier, looking up at the massive steel construction, says, "Jiminy Christmas I think this is it."

He bangs his head against the window, trying to see to the top of the emissions towers.

"In fact," he says, "I will bet you a dollar that this *is* it."

Blechhammer.

We've found it.

At the security entrance behind the first huge vat, a thick man in a black canvas jacket comes out of a little security booth and walks toward the idling samochódy.

The Bombardier bolts out of the backseat and marches up to this thick man. He has the old nylon escape map in his hand.

Bernadette and I simply watch for a moment as the Bombardier begins to tell his story to this thick man in a black canvas jacket.

We know we should want to remember this meeting, that this meeting is important, but we both feel weird.

"Why is it still here?" I say, "Why isn't it just a pile of rubble?"

Bernadette squeezes my hand and smiles at me weakly.

We don't know.

After observing the moment, I jog up to the Bombardier and this man. I have a tape recorder and microphone in my hands.

Maybe, I think, it will feel more profound later.

172

Later, I think, anything could feel profound, so try to remember and record.

Just as the Bombardier begins tracing the route with his finger on the road map, I reach them with the microphone.

I record the Bombardier saying "boom boom" very loudly and casting his hand into the air.

The security guard smiles cheerfully at this, exposing his thin, slightly crooked teeth.

The security guard narrows his black eyes behind his glasses and says something in Polish.

The Bombardier points at the map and says "boom boom" again, a little softer this time.

The security guard shrugs.

"Tak, tak," he says.

They stand looking at each other, and then a flash of recognition moves across the security guard's face.

He holds up his palm, then a finger.

He lumbers back inside his security booth to the phone there.

The factory feels empty of people, but the Bombardier and I, as we stand in the parking lot, can hear its oily parts humming.

"It was about noon in 1944 when we dropped our bombs," the Bombardier says, blowing into his hands to keep them warm.

"It's 12:04 now," I say.

Without thinking, we both look up.

The sky has only a few stringy clouds in it.

The security guard lumbers back to us in his black canvas coat, and he smiles again and shrugs.

"This is the place?" the Bombardier asks.

The security guard shrugs.

"Tak, tak," he says.

The Bombardier shakes the security guard's hand, and he walks back to his booth. We take some pictures of the emissions towers and the huge vats.

The Bombardier stamps his feet and blows into his hands for a minute or two, and then, because we can't think of anything else to do, we walk back to the samochódy and drive off.

Dear Luddie,

I'm afraid I haven't explained well enough about the hermit crab.

I'm afraid I haven't explained well enough because I can still see its black claws against the blue sky. I can still see the little hairs, the stringy clouds, the fading sun, the beach, the stick. I see it all so clearly every day, so I know I haven't explained well enough.

I see it so much that it's not just one hermit crab I killed, it's like a tower of hermit crabs in my memory, all flying out over the sea to die when I smash their shells with my stick.

Why did I kill them, Luddie?

I laughed and laughed when I did it.

My brother slapped me on my sunburnt back, and we ran up and down the beach with our stick, killing crabs.

I wonder, do you like the singing saw?

I think a dying hermit crab would sound like a singing saw if you could hear it when you smashed your stick against its shell.

Dear Luddie,

As we drive toward Krakow away from the synthetic oil factory in Brzeg, the Bombardier sits quietly in the backseat.

With the microphone in my hand, I ask him how he feels seeing Blechhammer again, but he waves me off.

I don't know why I brought this microphone and tape recorder. It seems so silly to me now, but when I packed them I had visions of serious reporting. It's clear there will be no serious reporting today, so I put the microphone and tape recorder away.

Bernadette and I don't know what to say to the Bombardier, so we sit in silence and look out the windows at your country.

Trying not to hear the singing saw, I look out the window and see that every house in your country has a fence, but every fence in your country comes from a different time.

Some fences are nineteenth-century wrought iron, others are picket-like. Some are chain-link and then others are old washing machine parts and junk wired together. All are different colors and heights, and all are right next to one another.

I see the roadside chickens and dogs of your country peck and sleep beside whatever fence there is, wrought iron or junk.

When we meet, Luddie, we should talk about your fences.

Besides fences, chickens, and dogs, I also see every tree has at least four or five bulby bushes clogging its branches.

"Mistletoe," Bernadette says.

"Really?" I say.

"It's like a tree virus," Bernadette says.

"Not very romantic," I say.

In the rearview mirror, I can see the Bombardier staring out the window, his floppy pink ears resting under his feathered hat.

We pass a group of people pruning their mistletoe-infested trees and burning the branches in big piles.

I give a little honk and wave, and the people look up, startled.

Every few miles, the air gets thick with this tangy char of burning branches.

When we see the smoke above the road, we open the windows to let the tangy char in.

Because the sky is still very clear and sunny and because we have gotten more used to spring in your country, Bernadette and I stick our arms out the windows as if it were summer in America. Bernadette and I make waves with our hands.

We have a few hours of this, driving with our arms out, making waves with our hands.

The Bombardier every so often says, "I've never seen such a poor, depressed country."

He slumps back in his seat.

"This looks like a tough town," he says as we wind our way around a decrepit traffic circle.

We try to cheer him up, but he is stuck in his gloom.

"The area between Wroclaw and Krakow," Bernadette says to the Bombardier after looking in the guidebook, "is the industrial part of Silesia, so it's bound to look a little rough."

The Bombardier nods and puts the stem of his glasses in his mouth, but he doesn't seem hopeful.

"Germany was a very clean country," he says, "even though they lost the war."

Dear Luddie,

As we drive into the city of Krakow, the Bombardier's gloomy mood begins to lift.

As we drive into the city of Krakow, he begins to tell more and more stories from the backseat, and the stories get better and better.

The sun has gone down behind us, and the lights of the city pulse ahead of us.

He tells us about driving his father's Model A Ford in the tall grass of the Midwest, about his first baseball game, his first drink, his first time in Russia.

"After the Allied plane picked me up from Rzeszów," the Bombardier says as we veer off the interstate toward the city of Krakow, "we were taken into a little Russian village.

"A few days after we arrived in this village," he says, "the Russian soldiers there had a big dance."

As I drive and as the Bombardier tells stories, your country turns from mistletoe trees and chickens to tall, box-like buildings and flashing neon signs.

"Unfortunately," the Bombardier says, as we drive by these buildings and signs, "there were only four or five girls in the village, so most of the men had to dance with other men at such a dance, which we understood was a weekly affair in this village.

"This meant, of course, that as new Americans, we were choice partners for the Russians, who had been dancing with each other for quite a while.

"These Russians," the Bombardier says as we cross a bridge into a teeming traffic circle, "were so obsessed with rank it was absurd.

"This obsession with rank even carried over into the dance.

"I was a captain, so I had to be paired with the Russian captain, even though the Russian captain was a huge burly man, completely wrong for me as a dance partner."

I step on the gas pedal to pass a little junk car.

"I got kind of looped on vodka," the Bombardier says with a laugh, "and this big Russian wanted to dance and dance."

In the backseat, we hear the Bombardier let out a gleeful little whinny, imitating his dancing and dancing.

"That man threw me around like a rag doll for hours," he laughs, "until finally his superior made him stop!

"Oh, I was so grateful!" the Bombardier says, his voice cracking with laughter. "I wanted to pat that colonel on the back!"

It's been a long day of driving, and that is part of why we laugh so hard at this story, but also, the little Bombardier and this big Russian.

Can you see them? The big hand with black hairs on its knuckles sliding around the Bombardier's waist? The Bombardier drunkenly trying to keep up with the twirling Russian?

They make a clear picture in a great story for us, so we're all laughing so hard we have tears in our eyes as we drive into Krakow.

Dear Luddie,

The samochódy sails into the center of Krakow after this story without any swerving, lumbering, or deep breaths.

We sail into the center of Krakow easily, without swerving, lumbering, or deep breaths, and we park the samochódy in the old stable behind our hotel.

Our hotel, which is in the shadow of Wawel Castle in Krakow, takes us in.

"All right kids!" the Bombardier says, standing stoutly in the doorway of our room in this hotel, "I'm taking you out for a fancy dinner here in Krakow, Poland. My treat!"

Bernadette and I feel silly, like we're on a game show, but we play along, clapping our hands excitedly and then changing into fancy dinner clothes.

We've made it to Krakow, where the pope hid from the Nazis in a little closet. The pope hid here, but no one hides now on a wet evening during a warm spring. No one hides because, as I'm sure you know, Luddie, Krakow on a wet evening during a warm spring is so beautiful.

No one hides.

We walk under Krakow's statues and through Krakow's streets to a fancy restaurant with the Bombardier, who is in a great mood, telling story after story.

We've all washed the day-long car trip from our bodies and we've changed into fancy dinner clothes. Bernadette is in a skirt, tights, and a sweater, I'm in a shirt tucked into trousers, and the Bombardier is in his wool suit and feathered hat.

We're no longer dimwitted travelers, but Americans with money out on the town.

It's very agreeable.

Dear Luddie,

The fancy restaurant serves me, Bernadette, and the Bombardier a fish baked in salt, a bowl of beet soup, and a steak, respectively, along with many glasses of beer all around.

The food is delicious, and the Bombardier says he doesn't feel so disappointed by Blechhammer now, because we still have Rzeszów to go.

We still have Rzeszów to go, where we may find the hideout, and where we may find you, Luddie.

Think of it!

The Bombardier doesn't say Rzeszów is where we may find you, Luddie, but we all know it, so we smile and eat our food joyously.

"Krakow certainly is a city, isn't it?" the Bombardier says, wiping his lips.

"You know," he says, "my wife was a city girl. She always loved cities, especially Chicago."

He puts down his forkful of meat.

"Her father," the Bombardier says, "worked for the Field Museum in Chicago as an engineer, but he never had anything more than an eighth-grade education."

"Mmm," I say, eating my fish.

"You know," the Bombardier says to Bernadette, "he helped to build the atomic bomb."

"Really?" Bernadette asks, scooping a bit of soup from her chin with her spoon.

"Yes," the Bombardier says, "He could put together anything at that Field Museum, and someone very important noticed this, so he got to work on the Manhattan Project down in New Mexico."

All around us in the fancy restaurant, people are chattering happily in Polish.

"After the war," the Bombardier says in his loud, clear English, "when his daughter and I married, he gave me an old hunk of metal as a present.

"I looked at this hunk of metal, and I said, 'Why, thank you sir,' and he smiled at me in a very peculiar way.

"He asked me if I knew what this hunk of metal was.

"Well, I turned it over in my hands, but for the life of me I couldn't tell it apart from any other hunk of metal, so I said, 'No, sir. I don't know what this is.'

"'It's a radio tower,' he said, 'from New Mexico.'

"He smiled again at me and I smiled back, still not quite sure what to make of it.

"'It's from the first atomic test down there, son. The bomb melted that radio tower down into this little hunk. I thought you might like to have it.'"

The piece of fish on my fork is quivering halfway between my plate and my mouth.

"Well, I certainly did like to have it! I still do have it to this day," the Bombardier said. "It's sitting there on my desk at home as we speak."

Bernadette chokes a little on her beer.

"You've had a radioactive hunk of metal," she says, coughing, "on your desk for fifty years?"

"Indeed I have," the Bombardier says, beaming.

I put my forkful of fish down.

"I'm sure," he says, "that it would set off—what do you call those things?—a Geiger counter?"

I put my forkful of fish down and think about the Bombardier's den and Geiger counters.

Bernadette looks at me with a strange kind of horror.

Dear Luddie,

I know a story I've never told the Bombardier or Bernadette. I know a story about the Bombardier's den and Geiger counters that I won't tell Bernadette or the Bombardier, but it's a true story so I will tell you, Luddie.

It's a true story so I will tell you, but please don't tell Bernadette or the Bombardier.

It's a story about the Bombardier's den and me as a boy when I was in fifth grade, stealing coins from his coin collection, and the hunk of metal.

I stole everything I could then—baseball cards, gum, balloons, golf balls, candy bars, magazines, tapes—anything and everything, including coins from the Bombardier's collection in his den.

I stole the coins and hid them in a paper sack with all my other stolen things, waiting for a day when I could do something with all of it, but what I would do I had no idea, so I just kept my sack full of stolen stuff hidden in the closet of the Bombardier's guest room.

At Christmastime that year, the Bombardier took me to the toy store to window shop.

There at the toy store I became frenzied, stealing matchbox cars, rubber balls, keychains, handcuffs, sticker books, and action figures, all while the Bombardier strolled down the aisles looking for a good Christmas present for me.

"What about this?" he asked, holding up a model airplane.

"No," he said, reconsidering, "too much."

As he walked around, I stuffed everything I could in my baggy parachute pants, and when we got back to the Bombardier's house, I stuffed some more.

I snuck into his den, and I took more of his coins and I took his watch, and I took his hunk of metal from on top of his desk.

I held the hunk of metal from on top of his desk in my little hand and I hefted it. It could be platinum, I thought, and then I stuffed it in my underwear.

It felt smooth and cold in my underwear, like falling.

As I walked I felt it wiggle out from its spot in my underwear, out from the leg hole and down to my ankle, where I had tucked the parachute pants into my sock.

I walked to the guest room with the metal swinging around my ankle, and in the guest room I hid everything in my paper sack in the closet. I took the hunk of metal out of my pants and hid it in a shoe. Then I went into the living room to watch old Superman and Home Run Derby reruns on cable.

Hours later, the Bombardier's radical daughter came in with the paper sack in one hand and the hunk of metal in the other.

She was going out on a date that night, so she had on lots of makeup and a shiny shirt.

"What the hell is this?" she asked, holding up the hunk of metal.

"I don't know," I said. "Platinum, maybe?"

She smelled nice.

She smelled nice, and I smelled her a lot when she threw the metal into the paper sack and then dumped everything in the sack out onto the floor between me and the TV.

Her smell was all over the room.

"What the hell," she said, "is all this?"

I kicked at a shiny pack of baseball cards that had landed near my foot.

"When I get home, you're going to be in big trouble, buster," she said, and pointed a red fingernail at me.

I scooped everything up and put it back in the sack and waited to be in big trouble, but I didn't get in big trouble because she didn't come home. Not that night, anyway.

When she did come home in the morning, she had forgotten all about the sack and the metal. Her makeup was still on and she still smelled sort of nice, but not as nice as before.

Dear Luddie,

At the dinner table in Krakow, the Bombardier winks at me and takes another bite of his steak.

Does he remember this story too?

"I bet you never knew what that was," he said to me, winking again.

I shake my head no and feel the cold metal trickling down my thigh.

"The atomic bomb," he says to Bernadette, "certainly is a contentious part of history."

Dear Luddie,

The Bombardier is a little drunk, and I wish he wouldn't talk about the atomic bomb.

The atomic bomb is the other side of the war.

The atomic bomb is the Pacific side, my father's side, Bernadette's mother's side.

I wish he wouldn't talk about it.

The atomic bomb is not the Bombardier's side of the war.

"The atomic bomb," Bernadette says to the Bombardier, "is on my mother's side of the war."

Our plates are clean except for a little bread and some brown spots of sauce.

"Your mother's side of the war?" the Bombardier asks, wiping his mouth.

It's clear to me he doesn't see a mother's side of the war. He sees the Pacific side of the war dimly, as the truly foreign side of the war, the mysterious womanly side. I watch him point out his chin and lick his lips free of sauce. There is a mother's side of the war though, even if the Bombardier doesn't see it. Bernadette sees it, and I don't know if the Bombardier wants to know what she sees.

"I know one is supposed to forgive," he says, dropping his napkin onto his plate, "but I've always said I will never forgive the Japanese."

I watch Bernadette wince when he says this.

She knows he couldn't have known her history, that he couldn't know enough to forgive. No one knows enough. The Bombardier doesn't know enough, and so he says he will never forgive. He says so, and I cringe.

He couldn't have known that Bernadette's grandmother on her mother's side was unforgivably Japanese since I haven't told him, and she hasn't told him, but when she winces I can see she had hoped he wouldn't be one of these men.

She knows all about these men from her mother's side of the war.

She knows all about these men because her grandmother on her mother's side married one of these men. She married an American man who could never forgive her.

That's her story.

It's a familiar story, an American story, and in it Bernadette's grandfather could not forgive his wife for her side of the war. And so our American history does not follow or favor the mother's side, only the father's side. It's only the brave soldier father's side that we know. It's the brave soldier's side we follow and succeed.

The mother's side sputters and faints, loses its name in the face of the father's side. There is no proper name for the mother's side, no succession, so what is to be done with the mother's side? How will its war be remembered?

Bernadette knows it won't be remembered, and she knows it's no one's fault but history's.

But she tells the story anyway.

"On my mother's side," Bernadette says to the Bombardier, "my grandmother was Japanese, in love with an American soldier at the end of her war. She married him."

Bernadette doesn't look at the Bombardier when she tells this story. She looks at her hands, and she looks at me.

I look at the Bombardier, and I see him let out a short and involuntary burst of breath as he listens.

I see his bottom lip jerk down and show his teeth. He is embarrassed, and embarrassed, he tries to say something, but he falters and instead motions to the waiter for another beer.

"My Japanese grandmother gave up her name with its unforgivable history," Bernadette says, flattening out her napkin on the table, "and she married an American soldier whose history had just been made."

"I'm sorry," the Bombardier manages to say.

His face is flushed.

"I didn't know you were," he begins, but stops. "I wouldn't have said it had I known."

"My grandmother," Bernadette says, still calm, rehearsed in her story, "left her unforgivable Japanese history and unforgivable family, and she moved to America, where she got two new names, a first and a last.

"She got her new last name from her husband, and her new first name from his church.

"'Honey,' the American pastor said to my grandmother in this American church, 'do you have a new American name you want? Or do you want me to choose one for you?'"

In Bernadette's telling, the American pastor has a honeyed drawl, a singsong voice.

"My grandmother didn't know the language in America," she says, "but she wanted a word for her, so she let the pastor choose her name.

"'Honey,' he said, 'how about Bernadette?'

"My grandmother didn't know. She already had a name. She got a new one.

"The American pastor sprinkled some holy water on her head and he said, 'Through you, Bernie, honey, may we see to forgive your people.'"

I watch the Bombardier sink into his seat.

He quietly sips his beer, but I can see him following the story, watching Bernadette's lips as she talks.

"My grandmother understood nothing in America," Bernadette says, "but she loved her brave soldier. She had no country, but she smiled and cried and looked up whenever anyone said 'Bernadette.'"

"Oh my," the Bombardier says, reaching out to touch Bernadette's hand.

"It's okay," Bernadette says, firmly, "I forgive you, but you have to listen to my story and stop interrupting."

"Of course," the Bombardier says, withdrawing his hand.

Bernadette pats his shoulder and smiles at him. I think she really does forgive him.

"This whole thing isn't about you, you know," she says and winks.

"I know," the Bombardier says.

Bernadette laughs.

"After a few years," she says, "my grandfather the brave soldier told my grandmother they were going to have a baby.

"Of course she knew already they were going to have a baby because she felt a rope in her stomach pulling her toward her home in the Pacific, but she knew her home in the Pacific was no longer there.

"'My home is here in America,' she said to her husband, 'My baby will be American.'

"Her brave soldier and her American pastor were very happy about this, that she had learned to say this in the American language.

"'Bernadette honey,' they said, 'you're such a smart girl!'

"When it came time, her baby was born American. It had light hair, pale skin, and it never spoke a word of Japanese.

"When her baby grew into a woman, it had a tall lanky American body. She looked all American as she grew up, except for her dark eyes."

I watch Bernadette think about the dark eyes. This is her story now.

"Her dark brown eyes held her mother's real name," Bernadette says, "but the Japanese disappeared from everything else. It was her mother's Japanese eyes she gave, eventually, to her own baby, along with that American name."

The Bombardier picks his hand up off the table and points at Bernadette. She nods.

"And I grew up as American as anyone else," Bernadette says, "in America with my soccer teams, beanbag chairs, and dancing, but unlike my mother, I have a little darker skin and a little darker hair. I'm a little darker, a little smaller, a little more Japanese. I don't know if this makes me more or less forgivable, but it is who I am."

"Bernadette," the Bombardier says, "I am sorry."

Bernadette takes his hand in hers and pats it with her thumb.

"It's okay," she says.

The table is quiet.

"A toast," I say finally, "to the mother's side."

Dear Luddie,

We drink, and all is forgiven.

All is forgiven, but the Bombardier is on my mother's side, so it's no feat of memory for me to toast its history. We're all right here in Krakow. In Krakow, no one hides.

It's my father's side I forget.

Dear Luddie,

It's my father's side that languishes in the Pacific with the atomic bomb, and as we drink to the mother's side, I can see Bernadette and the Bombardier are so involved in forgiveness they've forgotten to ask about my father's side.

I don't remind them.

My history is all screwed up because it is my mother's side I remember. It's my mother's side I toast and know, not my father's side.

I know the names and the history of the men on my mother's side, but on my father's side it's all lost, drowned in the Pacific or burned off in the wild blue yonder sunk in a drugged haze.

No one hides in Krakow.

My grandfather on my father's side died delivering the atomic bomb.

He died on the USS Indianapolis when he was twenty-four.

He died for his country when he was too young to have a history, when my father was just a baby too young to have a memory.

My father who took me to the beach with my brother who cut open a fish. My father who sat in the surf while we hit hermit crabs with a stick.

My father who flew off into the wild blue yonder with cocaine-filled shoes.

My father who called me in New England after September 11, after twenty years, to tell me not to join the fight.

"Don't die for your country, kid," he said to me, his voice rasping and strange. "Our family has already done that."

Our family, I thought.

Our family on my father's side, who were all in the Navy, dying, or in the swamp, dealing drugs, all killing what they had to kill in order to survive their history.

"Tell your brother hello," my father said to me.

I could hear him smoking somewhere.

"Tell him," my father said, "we don't need any more brave soldiers."

Dear Luddie,

"Who wants dessert?" I ask Bernadette and the Bombardier.

"Oh," Bernadette says, "me!"

"Sure thing," the Bombardier says, winking at me again, definitely drunk but thoroughly forgiven now, and so pleased.

At the fancy dinner table in Krakow, we eat chocolate cake and we drink sticky liqueur until we've forgotten all about the Japanese, my dad, the atomic bomb, and Blechhammer.

We walk back through the spring night of Krakow, full of food and beer and sticky liqueur, and the Bombardier asks, "Well, kids, what shall we do tomorrow?"

"Something great," Bernadette says and leans into my wool coat.

I think of our schedule, the day the airline took from us.

I feel a little sober.

"We should probably," I say, "go to Oświęcim."

"Ah," the Bombardier says cooly, "there is that."

"Where?" Bernadette asks, smiling up at me sweetly.

The Bombardier and I are quiet.

We feel a little sober.

"What's Oświęcim?" Bernadette asks again.

The Bombardier pulls his hat down a little.

"Auschwitz," he says.

Dear Luddie,

After stumbling into our hotel in the shadow of Wawel Castle, for the first time on this trip I fall into a fast sleep beside Bernadette.

I fall fast asleep and in my fast sleep, I drunkenly dream of my brother and me driving for days and days to a small town in the Midwest called Palestine.

In my dream, we drive for days and days to Palestine, where we see rows and rows of crumbling houses.

These rows of crumbling houses in Palestine have little gardens behind them and rusted-out cars and washing machines in front of them.

I dream the gardens have sticks in them, sticks tied together in crosses.

These crosses have old pink t-shirts stretched over them.

These are scarecrows in my dream, Luddie.

Hidden in these scarecrows, I dream I see a young woman, fifteen, standing on the side of the road as we drive into Palestine.

She stands down in the ditch beside the road, with one leg propped up toward the road, as if she is getting ready to run out of the ditch onto the road away from the pink-shirted scarecrows.

She stands there, looking down the road, swinging her arms in front of her and clapping her hands.

She watches us drive by.

She doesn't run out.

We drive by her, and we pull the car into a gravel parking lot by a lake in Palestine in this dream.

The lake smells so familiar, Luddie, like diesel and fish.

In my dream this is the town the Bombardier's great ancestor founded with his brothers.

Palestine.

In my dream, the Bombardier's great ancestor and his brothers are sons of a Quaker blacksmith, not the Captain's sons, and these blacksmith's sons found Palestine to sit in circles and to keep quiet.

In my dream my brother and I drive for days to get here.

We drive and drive and as we come close to Palestine in this dream, we see red-winged blackbirds on telephone wires, on fences, and in the ditches beside the road.

They perch everywhere like black smudges, then take flight with their brilliant wings flashing.

I hit one with the car, and I watch it tumble and die in the rear-view mirror.

My brother looks at me then, from the passenger seat. He has his high-school red hair flying full behind him from the open window of the car in the dream.

"Oh, I see," he says, so sadly. "You've taken me here to kill me."

Dear Luddie,

I have to tell you, your country loves some bad music.

I have to tell you your country loves American power ballads from the late '80s and early '90s, and these power ballads are some bad music.

In your country, we hear lots of Celine Dion and Whitney Houston, Luddie.

In your country, we hear "Love Is a Battlefield" by Pat Benatar and "We Don't Need Another Hero" by Tina Turner.

On a normal day, I would simply cringe or roll my eyes at these power ballads, but complex new meanings hover at the edges of these power ballads as I hear them in this new country as we ride on a rickety bus to Oświęcim, but these new meanings are too much for me to understand.

They are too much for me to understand because, I have to tell you, I am distracted by a picture the bus driver has pasted to his sun visor in your country.

The bus driver in your country has a cut-out picture of a woman's ass in a thong bikini taped to his sun visor.

It distracts me from the power ballads.

A fluorescent yellow thong. Two wet butt cheeks, Luddie.

The picture flaps in the wind from the bus driver's open window in your country.

"Is this how I mentally prepare to see the biggest cemetery in the world?" Bernadette asks me, "Listening to Pat Benatar and looking at a thonged ass?

"I feel like I'm on a middle-school field trip," she says, and slumps in her seat.

We're a little hungover.

I look out the window and try to breathe deep, but the landscape is no more of a comfort than Pat Benatar or the ass.

Small roadside bars decompose in the weeds, and a smattering of chickens and dogs roam through the mess of your country.

The bus lurches up a winding road toward the biggest cemetery in the world.

We've decided to go to the biggest cemetery in the world today because we don't have time for a leisurely day in Krakow. The airline took our leisurely day in Krakow, so we got up this morning and stumbled to this bus with the other tourists, hungover but determined to keep a schedule.

The Bombardier is fine, excited even, fully dressed and shaved, sitting ramrod straight in his seat on this bus.

We've decided to go to Oświęcim with the ramrod-straight Bombardier because we are so near it in our hotel in Krakow, and because it is a part of the war that the ramrod-straight Bombardier feels removed from.

"The Holocaust as we know it," he says to us, "didn't come to light until much later. During the war, when we flew over the camps in Poland and Austria and Germany, we only knew we weren't to bomb them. We had no idea what was happening there. No one did."

Dear Luddie,

Auschwitz.

Auschwitz was happening there, and "Auschwitz" is a word in my language.

It means suffering beyond articulation.

It means atrocity beyond imagining.

It means everything evil, and it means nothing real.

I say the word in airports, and I say the word in grocery stores, and I say the word in a rickety bus looking at a thonged ass.

I read it in books and I hear it in movies, and as I hear it and read it and say it, the spell of the word becomes broken.

The spell of the word "Auschwitz" becomes broken, and it no longer conjures any ghosts.

It no longer conjures any ghosts. It only conjures letters.

"Auschwitz," in my language, is a spelling bee word, a word to be typed fast in speeches and papers, but not a word to conjure any ghosts or cast any spells. Nothing succeeds it. The word is not agreeable.

The place itself, I hope and dread, will be different from the word.

I hope the place itself will be different because already I have found the place itself has this new name.

Oświęcim.

"Oświęcim" is a word in your language, Luddie, but I don't know what it means.

Dear Luddie,

I'm going to find out what it means, but I don't think I want to be Madame Psychosis today.

Today, my sweater has a hole in it. Today, I hear a crow click and caw outside the bus window, and I don't know what to do.

The sky is clear. I don't want to. Not today.

I don't want the dead to correspond with me today, Luddie.

Today, I think I would rather be the witness. Can I switch? Is this all a game? Is it all like the game Hot Lava my brother and I played when we were boys?

"The carpet is hot lava," we said. "Don't touch it!"

"You touched it! You touched it! Oh, it burns! It burns!"

It burns, but only until dinnertime. At dinnertime it doesn't burn. My brother and I run across the hot lava to the table as if it were just carpet at dinnertime.

Can today be like that game, Luddie? Can Bernadette be Madame Psychosis today? In her hungover mood it seems right, and I will be the witness today. I will watch everything and take note, untouched by the dead. Can I? Is this all a game? Do you mind?

Dear Luddie,

The Bombardier says, "Oświęcim is a tough town," as we ride by graffiti-covered bus stops and crumbling cement tenements on our way into the concentration camp.

Blocky apartment buildings rise above the scrubby pines, then fall away as we get to the parking lot of the camp.

Oświęcim is a tough town.

Pay attention.

The other tourists, Bernadette, the Bombardier, and I step off the bus and shuffle into the main entrance of the concentration camp, where we buy tickets and get a map.

With our tickets and our map, we sit in a small dark lobby with bottles of water and candy bars we buy from the snack bar.

Oświęcim is a tough town with tickets, maps, water, and candy bars.

"Have either of you two seen *The Passion?*" the Bombardier asks in the small dark lobby of Oświęcim.

Bernadette and I shake our heads.

"I've not seen it," the Bombardier says, "but I've heard it is an astute representation of Christ's final hours."

We sit silently.

A young woman weeps at the table beside us.

Our tour of the camp will start in a few minutes, the ticket-taker says, after a short film.

"The Russians, you know," the Bombardier says, adjusting the pin on his lapel, "were the first to reach Auschwitz."

He thinks for a moment.

"Yes," he says, "we know now that the Russians suffered tremendously during the war."

This is what happens, and after the Bombardier says this about the

Russians, and we eat our candy bars, we watch the film in a small theater beside the snack bar.

In a small theater beside the snack bar, we see Auschwitz as we've come to know it, with black-and-white bodies bulldozed into pits.

After we see the black-and-white bodies bulldozed into pits, we walk out of the dark theater into the hazy day of the concentration camp in Oświęcim.

One thing will lead to another here, and I will try to be the witness and watch it and take note. In time maybe one thing will lead to another and it will all make some sense, but for now one thing will simply lead to another, and I will watch it and take note. I am the witness today in Oświęcim.

The first thing I witness in Oświęcim is that, when we walk out into the hazy day, we walk under the gate that says "Arbeit Macht Frei."

I watch us go, and I take note.

Under the "Arbeit Macht Frei" gate, we see a tour group of Israeli teenagers walking toward us, down the main gravel path of the camp.

They walk down the main gravel path of the camp in Oświęcim, and they have blue and white Israeli flags and digital video cameras in their hands.

They walk past us with their flags and digital video cameras, recording themselves waving their flags in the camp, and they walk out of the camp under the "Arbeit Macht Frei" gate.

They are witnesses too.

It is a gray, slightly chilly spring day, hazy, and most of the leaves have not yet begun to bud on the trees in Oświęcim.

This is what happens.

We stand in a little group in front of our tour guide.

Our tour guide, a woman in middle age, looks like a diplomat.

She has short blonde-brown hair blown dry into an elaborate coif, and she has on noticeable makeup.

"Welcome," she says, "to Auschwitz."

The makeup is noticeable but not ostentatious. It is, I notice, heavy on the rouge.

She has on this noticeable, not ostentatious makeup, but she has such a serious look on her face that I can't imagine her applying any of this makeup. I can't imagine her getting out of bed in the morning, eating breakfast, or driving to work here in Oświęcim.

She is a professional.

She's wearing a white leather shirt and an elaborate wool poncho, plaid pants, and brown patent leather shoes.

I want to listen to her as she explains everything thoroughly, clearly, and precisely in English with a slight Polish accent.

She explains everything, and she seems empathetic and open to questions, but she does not solicit them.

As we walk down the gravel path toward one of the brick buildings in Oświęcim, the Bombardier asks her, "Where is the sign that reads, 'The Only Way to Escape is Through the Chimney'?"

The tour guide shakes her head.

"I'm sorry," she says, "but there is no such sign here in Oświęcim."

The Bombardier touches his hand to his chin.

He leans in to me and says, once she has turned around, "I could show you five U.S. history books that say there was such a sign at Auschwitz."

Very quietly he says, "Either my books are mistaken, or she is."

Dear Luddie,

We follow our tour guide into the rows of brick buildings in Oświęcim, and we see the sites of some of the war's worst horrors.

As we see the sites of some of the war's worst horrors, I stop being the witness for a minute. It's just a game anyway, so I stop being the witness, and I try to imagine our tour guide being seduced.

I try to picture her as a man pulls her behind a brick wall.

I try to picture her elaborate coif bobbing as he presses her poncho close to him.

I try to picture it, but my fantasy falls apart.

My fantasy falls apart as we walk along the gravel path and I think, surely even Oświęcim had seductions.

Or have I misunderstood everything?

I may have misunderstood everything, but right now it isn't important. What's important is watching and taking note of everything that happens to us here at Oświęcim.

What happens is I reach out to hold Bernadette's hand when we walk into more brick buildings, but she draws her hand back.

She's crying slightly.

What happens in this new brick building is that we stop in front of a wall.

On the wall hang framed drawings.

"They were made by a survivor," our tour guide tells us.

The Germans in these framed drawings all have cartoon barrel chests.

The prisoners in these framed drawings are all small and hunched over. Cartoons.

"The drawings show different scenes from the camp," our tour guide says, "such as roll call and a hanging."

I take pictures of the drawings, and then I take pictures of the little tile furnaces each room in this building has, then I follow our tour guide back out onto the path.

Another tour follows closely behind us, and in this tour the guide speaks in slightly accented French.

I drift between the tours, taking pictures of the drawings and the furnaces and the gravel path, recording what happens.

The brick buildings and the trees and the sky here in Oświęcim are austere and manicured.

If I weren't the witness, I would say the buildings and the trees and the sky are beautiful here in Oświęcim.

Everything is beautiful, clean, and preserved inside the camps at Oświęcim.

Inside the barracks building our tour guide, standing in front of framed photographs of victims, says the Allies knew of the Nazi concentration camp here in Oświęcim as early as 1942.

The Bombardier asks, "Was it bombed?"

"No," the tour guide says. "Only the oil factory was bombed."

"Blechhammer?" I ask, but no one hears me, so no one answers.

We walk on through the barracks to the beds where the workers slept.

The Bombardier says to Bernadette, "My dugout bed was almost like this."

He points to a rickety wooden bunk with a straw mattress.

The tour guide says, "The workers slept three or four to a bed in these barracks."

The Bombardier whispers to me, "We slept two to a bed."

I take a picture of one bed pushed up next to the glass.

After seeing the brick buildings, the drawings, the little furnaces, and the beds, we take a taxi to Birkenau, just outside of Oświęcim. We take a taxi to Birkenau to see where the crematoriums once stood.

Dear Luddie,

Birkenau is not Oświęcim, but Birkenau still requires a witness.

What is a witness?

A witness is a scientist.

At Birkenau I am the witness, and I watch and take note as the tour guide's thin lips tremble when she mentions the Hungarian Jews shipped in to the camp at the end of the war.

"So many Hungarian Jews were shipped in to the camp," she says and touches a wooden bench, "just at the end of the war."

Her lips tremble.

She leads us down below the wooden benches where the so-many Hungarian Jews sat, and we see the dank gas chambers.

In the dank gas chambers, our tour guide explains Zyklon B and concrete walls and the darkness.

We see the steel showerheads.

We see the heavy doors.

I take pictures of them.

I take pictures of the steel showerheads and the heavy doors, and then we walk out of the gas chambers, out into the day at Birkenau.

The tour ends in the guard tower where the Nazi soldiers once stood watching over the prisoners.

From this guard tower, we can see the old pine forests and the new housing developments surrounding the camp in Oświęcim a few miles away.

We can see the other tourists shuffling along the paths.

"At the end of this row of buildings," our tour guide says, "you can see where the two chimneys were."

We look down the row of buildings and see spaces where the trees don't grow.

"Where are the crematoriums now?" the Bombardier asks.

"The Nazis destroyed them," our tour guide says, "before the Russians could come and preserve them."

I look out at the spaces left by the destroyed chimneys and I try to imagine them, but a group of Italians has come up the stairs into the guard tower, and these Italians are rowdy, laughing and yelling.

A rowdy Italian child brushes past my legs in the guard tower.

I take more pictures because it is beautiful and then we take a taxi back to Oświęcim, where we wait for our bus back to Krakow.

Dear Luddie,

Outside the museum compound at Oświęcim, I kick at the gravel and walk up and down the driveway while the Bombardier comforts Bernadette.

She's crying hard now.

I am not crying because I am the witness, recording what happens here, and as the witness I observe the parts of the compound, the people, and the sky.

The sky is clear, the people are silent, and, a little ways down from the main museum, the parts of the compound are displayed on a giant black map from 1944.

The map shows the routes the victims took to get here.

Here, where the concentration camps sprung up like mushrooms for miles and miles.

White hash marks show the routes the victims took.

White death's heads show the concentration camps.

I follow the hash marks on this black map to a death's head near Koźle.

It's a white skull and crossbones on a black background and it sits over the name "Blechhammer."

I note that this white death's head "Blechhammer" is over a hundred kilometers away from Brzeg, where we saw the vats and emissions towers, where we took pictures and looked at the sky.

I rest my fingers on this white death's head.

I walk into the gift shop beside the map and ask the young woman behind the counter about this "Blechhammer," but she only shrugs and points me to a coffee-table book with a list of all the camps inside it.

There, I find a description of the death's head "Blechhammer," but no pictures.

"Blechhammer," the description reads, "was an Auschwitz subcamp seventy kilometers from Oświęcim, near the town of Koźle."

I walk over to the Bombardier and Bernadette.

"'Blechhammer was an Auschwitz subcamp seventy kilometers from Oświęcim,'" I say, "'near the town of Koźle.'"

The Bombardier frowns and Bernadette looks up at me with glassy eyes.

"No," the Bombardier says, "I remember we opened the bomb-bay doors over Opole, so it couldn't have been near Koźle."

"Come look at the map," I say, and we all walk along the gravel path to the black map with the white death's heads on it.

A group of teenagers sits on the curb beside the map, eating ice cream.

The Bombardier traces the white hash marks with his finger. The skin hangs from his knuckle like a drape.

"Our intelligence was so weak then," he says.

Beside the map, a teenager in a puffy coat lines his tongue along the base of his wobbly ice cream.

"What we were told," the Bombardier says, "was that Blechhammer was just an oil refinery near Brzeg."

"But what about this?" I ask, patting the white death's head on the black map with my palm.

"The Allied officers must have thought the oil refinery was part of the camp," Bernadette says, "or maybe 'Blechhammer' became the name of the oil refinery by mistake."

The Bombardier touches the death's head with his fingers.

"I'm sure my Blechhammer has no connection to a concentration camp," he says.

"I wonder what it was we saw in Brzeg," Bernadette says, wiping her eyes, "if it wasn't your Blechhammer?"

"It was," the Bombardier says, turning away.

Dear Luddie,

We ride back from Oświęcim in silence on a rickety bus.

There is no Pat Benatar, no Tina Turner, no ass, only the sound of the engine and three young American backpackers sitting behind us.

I can see these three young American backpackers in the wide rearview mirror at the front of the bus and, even though we aren't in Oświęcim, I still feel like being the witness. I still want to watch and take note.

"Did you notice," one of the young American backpackers says, "how much they talked about the Russians in there?"

This backpacker, I see, is a pasty one, with a polo shirt on and thick, black-rimmed glasses.

"It's that old Eastern Bloc mentality," he says, wiping his hands on his jeans, "still with the propaganda."

Another backpacker, a young woman with a long skirt and a thick cowry shell necklace, says, "Yeah, well you can't believe anything they tell you in there. It's all political."

In the rearview mirror, I watch her run her fingers along the part in the center of her head.

She sighs.

"Man oh man," the third backpacker says, "I'm just glad it's over."

This backpacker is big.

He looks like a football player, meaty and flushed.

The pasty backpacker and the cowry shell backpacker laugh.

"I mean," the football player says, "didn't you feel like burning the whole place down or something? Just to stop all of that . . ."

I watch him search for a word. His thick fingers twitch.

". . . all of that *stuff* from coming at you?"

"No doubt," the cowry girl says, "No doubt. It really is too much."

"But the Russians," the pasty one says, very serious, "the Russians brainwashed the Polish people. You can't trust them. You really can't. And the Jews . . ."

He lowers his voice and adjusts his glasses.

"I'm not anti-Semitic or anything, but the Jews want everyone to believe that they're the only ones who died in there."

"Yeah," the cowry girl says, "no one ever says anything about the gypsies."

"Have you guys been to Prague?" the football player asks.

"Oh my god, yes!" the cowry shell girl says. "Prague is so awesome!"

"The beer is so cheap," the football player says in awe.

I watch him think about the cheap beer. His eyes grow wide.

"Where did you stay?" she asks him.

"Some hostel," he says, waving his fat hand.

"No curfew?"

"None."

"Sweet."

"Can you believe," the pasty one interjects, "they had the shoes?"

The football player screws up his meaty face.

"Shoes?" he asks, "In Prague?"

To the left of the meaty football player, I can see the Bombardier's hat in the rearview mirror.

It slowly descends toward the window beside him.

Just as it is about to bang against the window the hat jerks up, only to slowly descend again.

He is dozing.

"The shoes," the pasty one says again, "they had all those shoes of the dead kids in that room. Did you see it?"

"Oh," the football player says, "we're back in there."

"It's so trite," the pasty one says.

"And the combs?" the cowry girl says.

215

"Totally gross," the football player says, smiling at the cowry girl.

Bernadette turns in her seat and gives me a deadly look. She truly is Madame Psychosis today.

"I know," I whisper, "but it's how they feel."

"They're fucking idiots," Bernadette says loudly.

The Bombardier's hat jerks up.

The three backpackers stop talking.

I watch them all look at one another.

"What's her problem?" the cowry girl asks.

The other two grumble, but quietly.

"Where are you staying tonight?" the football player asks the cowry girl, and then they're off in another conversation.

Bernadette slumps back into her seat, eyes welling with tears.

"It's better to observe," I say to Bernadette.

She says nothing, but I can feel her imagination blooming with punishment for these backpackers. We say nothing, though. We just sit in silence on the rickety bus.

Dear Luddie,

I've written down all my notes from Oświęcim, and now I don't think I can sleep.

I don't think I can sleep, so I stare at the vaulted ceiling, the thickly painted wall, and I flop my leg out from under the covers, then I slide it back.

I've witnessed a lot.

I don't think I can sleep after witnessing so much, but I do sleep, and when I do sleep I dream in short, hard bursts.

In short, hard bursts I dream something happens to me, and I don't recover myself.

I dream in green waves.

I dream the screen changes in green waves, and a colossal hump grows in my backyard where the leaves won't fall.

I dream sore elbows pop and burst with fish-filled polyps.

I dream tea trucks collide on street corners, where silvery flophouse matrons lie supine on wooden benches, waving teeny flags.

I dream a chrome vulture pecks my neck until it has my voice in its beak. It speaks and says, "Sordid hot pins make sly ghosts," and I dream I know what this means.

I dream carrots grow from foreheads of singers and dangle down, away from the eyes.

I dream serenades from the mouths of caves roll over me as I lie paralyzed on a beach of orange sand.

I dream small-eyed guinea fowl fly from the trees above my broken-down wagon.

I dream I shit the tip or the tail of some beast into the laundry.

I dream, and then I start from sleep with a sleeve of sweat over my body, and I get up, and I walk the halls until the night is over.

Dear Luddie,

A witness watches and takes note but feels nothing, I think. A witness doesn't dream. A witness doesn't have short, hard bursts.

Dear Luddie,

Something is wrong this morning.

I feel it.

Something is wrong, but as I walk down the hallway to the Bombardier's room I don't know what it is. A witness observes without imagination, I think. A witness is pure sense.

I hear a warble and a screech.

Something is wrong.

I hear a warble and a screech, and I see the Bombardier coming out of his room, closing his heavy wooden door just as I round the corner.

I hear the warble and screech get louder when he turns to me.

"This is wrong," I think, and feel my heart beat.

A witness can't help. A witness can only observe, I think. A witness is pure sense, no feeling.

The Bombardier shuts his heavy wooden door calmly and turns to face me as I run up to him, heart beating.

When he turns, I see one of his flesh-colored hearing aids dangling out of his left ear. It is feeding back horribly, screeching.

"All right my boy," he says with a big smile, "are you ready to find that dugout?"

He doesn't notice the dangling hearing aid, and I can't tell him about it.

I want to be the witness, Luddie, so I say nothing.

With the horrible warbling echoing around us, we walk down the hallway.

Bernadette meets us at the samochódy, bleary-eyed but with the road map and a cup of tea in her hand.

"Good morning, my dear," the Bombardier says, opening her door for her.

"What's wrong with your ear?" she says, sliding into the seat.

"What?" he says.

Cautiously, he glides his hand up to his ear.

We watch him gingerly touch the dangling plastic.

"Oh my," he says and shoves the dangling plastic back in his ear.

The warbling stops. The screeching stops.

Bernadette shakes her head sadly at me, and we all settle into the samochódy.

"I couldn't tell him," I say, cranking the engine.

She says nothing, just sips her tea.

Bernadette sips her tea and is silent, and as we drive, I am silent too.

I am silent because I am not too stupid to know my dreams have interfered with my science. My dreams have interfered with my science of witness, Luddie, so now I feel caught. I feel caught between observation and imagination, so I am silent.

Dear Luddie,

For two hours, as we drive down another bumpy two-lane Polish highway toward Rzeszów, I am silent, and I try to separate Oświęcim from fish-filled polyps.

Was the map of the camp real, I wonder, or was the map of the camp part of a dream?

The death's heads? The grassy hump?

What did I witness, and what did I dream?

I can't tell, but, I think, surely the map was real.

Surely it was real because I wrote it down in my letter to you, Luddie. I wrote it down in my letter after I was the witness, and what I wrote down in that letter to you were the real, noted things.

I wrote them down in my letter to you, but Bernadette, the Bombardier, and I didn't talk about them. We just rode the rickety bus back to Krakow in silence, as if we wouldn't talk about what we saw in Oświęcim. As if the trip to Oświęcim wasn't real.

"Rzeszów was just a tiny town," the Bombardier says from the backseat, "with only a few dirt roads and a small church."

He is cheerful, smiling and fidgeting there in the backseat.

"We held on as long as we could in the air, but with the pilot's leg injured as it was, we had to crash in Rzeszów," he says. "Our only other option would have been to jump, but to jump you had to fall from the bomb-bay doors and trust your parachute.

"Oh no," the Bombardier says, slapping his palms on his thighs, "I wasn't ready for that! So we held on in all that acrid smoke and guided her down."

The road gives a light buzz to my hands on the steering wheel, but the friction is no more jarring than that.

"We certainly were frightened there in Rzeszów," the Bombardier says, "but everyone we met was terribly nice."

Bernadette sits in the passenger seat, studying the road map and the atlas.

She angles the road map so I can see it, pointing at the big pink industrial blob marked "Rzeszów."

"They say it's grown quite a bit," the Bombardier says, "but I remember it was such a small village when we were there."

Dear Luddie,

An hour later, the rolling Polish countryside begins to clot with blocky buildings. More and more little cars zip past our samochódy the closer we get to Rzeszów, and my knuckles get a little whiter on the steering wheel.

Bernadette looks at me gravely.

Her dark eyes look sunk.

The blocky buildings grow and grow around the samochódy, my knuckles get whiter and whiter, and then we crest a hill and see down in the valley a huge industrial city.

Down in the valley we see Rzeszów, and we see it is not a small village.

The samochódy dips down into the valley at a steep angle, and I feel yellow ropes tug my stomach.

"Oh boy," the Bombardier says, "this little village certainly has grown up!"

With white knuckles and a tugging stomach, I steer the samochódy into the grown-up village of Rzeszów, with the Bombardier silently watching out the window with his index finger on his bottom lip.

He doesn't crash into Rzeszów this time, Luddie.

This time he just says "oh boy" as we crest the hill.

In Rzeszów, the huge industrial city, we just park the samochódy by a towering monument.

We leave the samochódy without cuts or bruises or legs to be cut off with pocketknives, and we study the monument, a bronze Liberty brandishing a torch for the fallen Polish soldiers of World War 1.

"Well," the Bombardier says, touching the bronze folds of the statue's dress, "I certainly don't remember her!"

The Bombardier and Bernadette, uncut and unbruised, begin to walk from this bronze Liberty toward the city center, but I stay.

I stay a second, and I look up at the sky, and I say to myself, "We are in your city, Luddie."

Do you hear me?

"Are you okay?" Bernadette yells, already down the road.

I nod because I am okay, but I am still caught.

I am still caught between my dreams and my observations. I am caught even here in your city, Luddie, when I should be the clearest correspondent or the clearest witness I can be. What should we do with these things in our brains we didn't live through? With what we've dreamed?

This is your city, where I will give you your letters, where you will read them, but my head is not clear. My head is not clear because I keep seeing white hash marks and black maps and grassy humps and flying fortresses and shitty laundry.

Something is wrong, Luddie, but I can't find my way through my observations and my imagination to figure it out.

Dear Luddie,

Bernadette, the Bombardier, and I wind our way from this bronze Liberty in your city to a spot where the map says a tourism office should be.

Off to the east, I can see cobblestone streets leading to a pedestrian mall with flags and little shops.

To the west, I can see miles of apartment buildings and factories.

"They must have put in cobblestones after the war," the Bombardier says, kicking at a stone with his boot.

Bernadette shakes her head.

She knows sixty years has many nights.

She knows sixty years has many nights over which the Communists could have built anything, but she knows even in sixty years of nights new cobblestones are unlikely.

I look around at grimy storefront after grimy storefront until I see a little sign that says in English "Office of Tourism."

In this grimy storefront amongst many other grimy storefronts in your city, a young woman in a purple and white windbreaker greets us.

"Welcome to Rzeszów," the young woman in the purple and white windbreaker says.

"Sit, sit," she says, pointing to some stools to her left, under a map of your city.

"Now," she says, smiling, "why are you here in Rzeszów?"

With a deliberate flourish, the Bombardier shows this young woman your photograph, Luddie, and this young woman says, "Ahhh."

"This is why we are here," the Bombardier says.

The young woman strokes your black-and-white face, then turns your photograph over.

"Ahhh," she says again, and yellow ropes pull my heart up.

I try to ignore them. I try to simply watch and take note, but I think she knows your street, Luddie, and this sends my mind into the clouds.

I feel time crumpling around me as the young woman in the purple and white windbreaker tries to find your street in her files. She's trying to find your street in her files and on her maps, but she has stopped saying "ahhh" and has begun to frown.

She can't find your street.

She frowns more severely.

I take note.

"This street," she says to the Bombardier, "does not exist in Rzeszów. I'm sorry."

The Bombardier touches his chin.

"Has this street," Bernadette asks, "ever existed in Rzeszów?"

The yellow ropes around my heart have gone a little slack.

The young woman looks at her map and shakes her head no.

"We stayed in a dugout, a little hole in the ground with woodburning stoves," the Bombardier explains.

The young woman nods and smiles.

"Do you know," the Bombardier asks, "where this dugout might have been?"

The young woman's face empties for a moment, then fills with some twisting of amusement and pity.

She glances at me with her twisting.

"I'm sorry," she says. "I don't think I can help you."

The Bombardier starts to speak but stops and touches his hat.

"Do you see this building across the street?" the young woman asks, pointing out the window to a fat concrete block with Polish flags waving over its doors.

"They might know something," she says. "There they may help you."

228

She smiles at us and presses her hands flat on her desk.

"Okay," she says.

"Thank you," Bernadette says, and we walk out into the huge industrial city of Rzeszów.

Dear Luddie,

The fat concrete block with Polish flags waving over its doors sits silent and dark across the main avenue.

"Surely," I say, "they will have records there."

The yellow ropes pull taut on my heart and stomach, but I feel strangely scared, Luddie.

I don't want to go into that fat concrete block.

"Before we go to that place," the Bombardier says, pointing at the building, "why don't we get some lunch."

Bernadette looks up into the sky.

I imagine falling out of the bomb-bay doors over this city, curling into a ball and plummeting into the fat concrete block like an axe flung into a birthday cake.

"Why don't we," Bernadette says. "I'm starving."

Instead of crossing the avenue to the fat concrete block, we walk east up the cobblestones to find lunch.

East up the cobblestones at the city center, we find a restaurant called Sphinx.

It has a plastic, noseless face hanging over the glass entrance doors.

"I remember," the Bombardier says, "seeing a Sphinx in Wroclaw."

"I think," I say, "I saw one in Krakow too."

"It must be a chain," Bernadette says, pushing through the glass doors under the plastic, noseless face.

At this Polish food chain, Sphinx, we sit quietly in our booth, listening to the house stereo play American power ballads.

"My heart," the stereo says, "will go on."

In this place, I order fish and chips, the Bombardier orders a hamburger, and Bernadette orders a Caesar salad.

"Can I borrow this?" the waiter asks after he brings our food, pointing at my guidebook.

"Tak, tak," I say and hand it up to him.

He takes it from me and skips over to the rest of the waitstaff, who stand expectantly around the hostess's lectern.

They giggle and point at the guidebook, then look over at us in amusement.

"Rzeszów must not get so many tourists now," the Bombardier says, poking at his hamburger. "It certainly didn't sixty years ago."

"I wonder," Bernadette says, poking at her salad, "how many bombardiers fell from the sky here?"

She nibbles a crouton and looks out the window.

"Do you think," she says, "Luddie saw you from her house?"

I crane my neck to look out the window and think I see the Flying Fortresses up there in the sky, in their v. The small black German fighters pursuing them. The one Flying Fortress breaking off from formation, diving down nose first, spiraling smoke behind it.

"It is a tragedy to grow old," the Bombardier says. "It's a tragedy to grow old and not be able to hear or see."

Bernadette and I wait for him to laugh, but he doesn't laugh.

He doesn't laugh about not being able to hear or see, he just pushes his plate away.

Dear Luddie,

When you were a small piece of orange light, I held you in my blue-veined arms.

Dear Luddie,

Full of bar food, we trudge through the warm spring day to the fat concrete block.

I shake my head to clear it, but the yellow ropes are pulling hard, mixing my mind.

We walk under the Polish flags, through the glass double doors, into the concrete block.

In the concrete block a man in a green wool suit stands idly behind a blocky counter.

We ask this man in a green wool suit about Rzeszów and dugouts and you.

We ask this man in a green wool suit at the counter in the fat concrete block, but he doesn't speak English, so he talks into his walkie-talkie and other men in identical green wool suits appear in the concrete block.

These men in green wool suits all jabber in rapid Polish into more walkie-talkies and guide us deeper into the fat concrete block.

They guide us to a room marked in red Polish letters.

All the men jabber in Polish and point at your picture as we walk into the room marked in red Polish letters.

These are the men of your country, Luddie, and they have normal faces and normal smells.

These are the normal men of your country, and we have finally found them in this fat concrete block.

One of these normal men in a green wool suit emerges from the others deep in the room.

This man says, "Hello."

This man's English is clear and crisp, with a slight British lilt to it.

This man has a wide, ruddy face, blue eyes, and a big moustache.

233

He sweats into his green wool suit because it's hot deep in the concrete block on this warm spring day. His moustache is damp.

He speaks to us in his lilting British English.

"You want to find a Ludwika Bandolac in Rzeszów?" he asks, nodding.

His walkie-talkie crackles.

"You want to find this street?" he asks, pointing at the back of your photograph.

"Tak, tak," I say, clapping my hands.

"Tak, then," this man says with a smile.

This man in green wool with a damp moustache then waves us along, rushing us from one end of a long hallway to the other, trying to help us find you and your street.

He rushes us deeper into the concrete block, into a back room, into a small office where he asks us to wait.

"You will wait here, yes?" he asks, "I will find your friend?"

"Tak tak," we all say and sit in the small office.

It has a strange, leather-lined door.

It's humid and hot.

After we sit down in the small office, the man in green wool rushes out of the leather-lined door, then he rushes back in.

The room is like a locker room for information, a sweaty humid place. He grasps his sweaty chin and chews his damp moustache as he stares at a map of the city hung on the wall near the leather-lined door.

He looks at your address on your photograph, and then he looks back at the map.

Finally, he calls the Bombardier over and rests a sweaty hand on the Bombardier's shoulder.

I watch the man try to tell the Bombardier something, but I can see the Bombardier can't understand.

I feel tiny pinpricks of sweat bleeding out of my pores. The heat is like a wool hat pulled over my face.

The Bombardier, I see, can't understand, even though he has leaned his floppy pink ear in so far it nearly rests on the man's lips.

The man in the green wool suit takes a step back and looks over at Bernadette.

Waving her over, he sends the Bombardier away with a push.

I start to follow Bernadette, but the Bombardier takes me by the arm.

His hat has been pushed back to the top of his head, and I can see drops of sweat glistening on his forehead.

He rubs a hand over his face, and I can hear his white stubble bristle.

"What did he say?" I ask, fighting to free my arm.

"It's a tragedy," the Bombardier says, "to not be able to hear or see."

His eyes hardly move behind his glasses.

"It's a tragedy to grow old," he says, his breath rasping.

What can I do, Luddie?

I stop fighting to free my arm and guide him to a chair by the leather-lined door below the map.

From our chairs I can just barely see Bernadette, who is talking with the man in the green wool suit.

I try to watch them out of the corner of my eye and take note.

"As a boy," the Bombardier says, patting my arm, "I heard everything."

The man has put his hand on Bernadette's shoulder.

She shakes her head.

"My mother would send me outside," the Bombardier says, "so she could talk with her sister in the kitchen, but even outside I could still hear them so clearly."

The man is pointing at the picture, putting his palm up, then laying it down flat with a sweeping motion.

235

"They talked about me every day in that kitchen, and I would sit so far away from them on a tree stump and hear every word."

Bernadette shakes her head again, and the man pats her arm.

"We lived in Kosciusko County, you know, named after the famous Pole. Our neighbors in Kosciusko County had the face of this famous Pole painted on their barn. Oh how I hated that face! At night I would sneak out and scribble all over this face with charcoal. He had such a spiky red beard, I couldn't resist. Boy, was I trouble!"

The Bombardier stamps his foot and claps his hands.

This is a new story.

I look away from Bernadette and the man, and I look at the Bombardier.

This is a new story. I've never known of the Bombardier as trouble.

Even when I thought of him as a child, I thought of him like the radical daughter thought of him, as the straightest arrow.

"Really?" I ask, "Trouble?"

"Oh yes," the Bombardier says, "I was quite the delinquent as a child."

"Really?" I say again.

"Really," he says with a smile and a wink. "It is quite remarkable I turned out at all."

Bernadette's voice echoes in this hot, humid concrete block.

"C'mon," she says, "we have to go."

"What did he say?" I ask.

Her eyes look strange.

"Nothing," she says. "Luddie isn't here."

"Not here?" the Bombardier asks, pulling his hat back properly onto his head.

"No," Bernadette says, "the man says she was not here. She was in Trzebownisku, a little village east of here."

"Trzebownisku," the Bombardier echoes.

"Does that sound familiar?" I ask.

"Why," the Bombardier says, "I think I have heard of it."

He smiles and touches his hat.

"Well, I'll be," he says.

"What is it?" I ask.

"I always thought we were in Rzeszów," he says.

"But you weren't?" I ask.

"I suppose not," he says.

"Well," Bernadette says, "let's go then before it gets too late."

Dear Luddie,
And you stayed there, leaving your body through mine.

Dear Luddie,

We follow the smallest, bumpiest two-lane highway across the river to Trzebownisku.

"The dugout," the Bombardier says, as we bump along, "was just a hole in the ground with two woodburning stoves and some beds."

In the rearview mirror, I watch him touch his fingers to the glass of his window.

"Panya and Maya," he says to no one.

"What do you think Luddie will look like now?" I ask.

"Well," the Bombardier says, "you've seen how she was. Quite beautiful. She had such a full laugh. Even in those times."

Bernadette starts to say something.

I see her mouth open and her tongue push forward, but she stops.

"I can almost hear it," the Bombardier says.

Bernadette reaches out and pulls my hand off the steering wheel, squeezing it instead of speaking.

"We are having an adventure," I say to her and smile.

And we are.

We are having an adventure, Luddie, coming to Trzebownisku to find you as witnesses or correspondents or bombardiers. The ropes have come back and pulled my insides up into their yellow light.

The sun has begun to set in our adventure, and this setting sun has drawn soft colors out of everything we see as we drive into your village.

The sun draws soft colors out of the grassy hills, the wooden fences, the dogs, and the chickens of your village.

The sun draws soft colors out of the bumpy road.

"Does any of this look familiar?" I ask the Bombardier.

"Well," he says, surveying the grassy hills, wooden fences, dogs, and chickens, "I don't remember."

Soft colors on a church and a small schoolhouse.

"This might be the church," the Bombardier says faintly, "that Renaldo went to."

Bernadette looks at me.

"Renaldo?" I say, but he doesn't answer.

The doors of the church are open so I pull the samochódy into the gravel parking lot.

"This might be the church," the Bombardier says again and jumps out of the samochódy.

He strides into the open doors of the church, but Bernadette and I don't follow.

We stand in the parking lot.

She looks down at the soft colors on the gravel parking lot.

"What did the man in the green wool suit tell you?" I ask.

"He said Luddie wasn't there. Not in Rzeszów," she says, kicking at the gravel.

"So she's been here the whole time?" I ask, but Bernadette doesn't tell me.

She doesn't tell me, she just grabs my hand and leads me across the gravel parking lot to the small schoolhouse.

I'm confused, but I'm excited, Luddie, because we are having an adventure.

I feel the fading sunlight drawing soft colors from the back of my neck as we walk, and then, as we enter the schoolhouse, I feel the soft colors fade.

The linoleum floor in the schoolhouse echoes with the slaps of small shoes, and we listen but we see nothing.

We see nothing but hear the echoes, and then we see ten kids, all holding hands in a line, marching from one room to another through the entryway where we stand.

Their slapping shoes echo around us.

The first one, a little blonde girl, squeals at us, and her shoe slaps echo faster across the linoleum.

The other echoes follow.

Her teacher, at the end of the marching chain, shoos the rest of the wide-eyed squealing kids into their next room and approaches us.

It's a mess of echoes.

We smile.

The teacher smiles.

We speak.

The teacher speaks.

No one understands anything.

The first little girl peeks around the corner of her new room.

I wave.

She squeals.

Our big shoes echo across the linoleum, back out into the sunlight.

"This is the schoolhouse in her village," Bernadette says to me as we walk, "and in it we found echoes and little girls."

Is this what a witness would say, or what Madame Psychosis would say? I'm not sure who is who anymore, Luddie. I'm a little confused.

"Echoes and girls," I say.

In the parking lot, we see the Bombardier is back in the samochódy.

The Bombardier is still the Bombardier.

"Any luck?" I ask him, climbing into the driver's seat.

"No luck," he says, and we drive on.

We drive on further down the road in your village, and further down the road we see a three-story wooden building.

It has a Polish sign above its double doors and a framed map in its parking lot.

"The town hall?" I say.

"The town hall of this little village," the Bombardier says remotely, "yes."

"Trzebownisku," Bernadette says.

The shadows stretch across the little junk cars in the parking lot of this town hall.

The shadows stretch across a few people leaving the town hall, walking to their little junk cars, looking at us strangely.

No one speaks English, but these few people follow us back into the town hall, casting long shadows in front of us.

Inside the town hall, the receptionist speaks to us in a flurry of Polish and points at the few people who have followed us in.

The receptionist has curly brown hair and a string of fake pearls.

She speaks to us in a flurry of Polish and other women drift out from other rooms in the town hall.

They crowd around us, pointing and arguing in their dresses and skirts.

We try to tell our stories, but no one understands.

The Bombardier pulls your photograph from his pocket, Luddie, and he points to your name.

The women gasp and take the photograph in their papery hands.

The women argue in Polish flurries.

Finally, the women frown, shake their heads, and shrug, their flurries over as quickly as they began.

The Bombardier takes the photograph back and turns to leave.

"Maybe we can still find that dugout," he says with a grim tone, and Bernadette and I turn to follow him, but just as we do a man comes rushing down the stairs.

This man is short, chubby, with red cheeks and a moustache.

The women talk excitedly again as this man strides forward to shake my hand.

"Hello," he says in clear English.

"Hello!" I say.

"Hello!" the Bombardier says and reaches in to shake the man's hand too.

The Bombardier tells this man his story in English, and the man sounds as if he understands.

This man says "uh huh uh huh uh huh" and he nods vigorously.

"And then we stayed in a dugout with Panya and Maya somewhere near here," the Bombardier says, pointing out into the long shadows, "and Luddie helped us so much. She's why we're here and this is her village."

The man says "uh huh uh huh uh huh" and nods vigorously.

He nods and directs a flurry of Polish back at the women who all stand around us.

They gasp again.

They burst into more flurries of Polish, and the man listens.

He frowns.

I hate to see this frown on the people in your country Luddie, because this frown only means our story has become confused.

"I'm sorry," this man says, too quickly I think. "There is no street here. There is no dugout."

He hands your photograph back to the Bombardier.

"There is no Luddie here," he says.

The yellow ropes on my heart and the yellow ropes on my stomach go slack.

I feel them drift from their point in the sky and fall like long shadows around me.

243

"Are you sure?" I ask.

"I'm sorry," he says, "I have lived here all my life. I know the streets. I know the names."

His hand pats the Bombardier's shoulder.

"There are many stories like this," he says and touches your photograph.

The Bombardier does not give up.

The Bombardier tells his story again to this man, in more detail this time, and this man says "uh huh uh huh uh huh" and nods vigorously again, but finally, after more frowns and shrugs and nods, it's final.

There is no street. There is no dugout. There is no Luddie.

"But we've traveled so far," I say, and as I say it I know it is stupid.

The man shrugs his shoulders and raises his eyebrows.

I take a step toward him, but I don't know why.

What do I want from him?

I want him to take pity on us, I think. I want him to tell us it has all been a game. This whole trip has been a game, and even though we didn't win this game, we performed admirably, and so he will give us a little prize anyway. This is what I want. Like a little boy, I want a little prize, but this man has no prizes. It is not a game. It burns.

Dear Luddie,

We leave this man and these women in this town hall.

We leave this man and these women in this town hall, and we walk out into the parking lot, away from this man and these women and into the air outside.

The air outside is suffused with spring smells and soft colors.

The soft colors have fallen into the long shadows, past the samochódy, onto the town hall.

The long shadows have almost turned into night, so we know we can't stay.

We know we must drive the samochódy back to Krakow.

We must drive the samochódy back to Krakow with nothing.

"I'm sorry," Bernadette says to the Bombardier.

"Oh," the Bombardier says, "it's not your fault."

He settles into the backseat of the samochódy with a sigh.

"We just should have planned better, I guess," he says.

"I'm sorry," I say, starting the engine.

"I sure wish," he says, "we could have found that damn hole in the ground."

"Maybe we can find some more information in Krakow," I say, "and come back."

We're bumping along the highway toward Rzeszów.

"No," the Bombardier says, "tomorrow we must start back for Berlin."

He rubs his hand over his mouth.

"It's over," he says.

We ride in silence along the bumpy highway back across the river.

The Bombardier turns to look at the lights of Rzeszów as we pass them, and as he does, his hat bangs against the window and falls into his lap.

10

Dear Luddie,

I have to tell you something, but I don't want to do it.

I don't want to do it because I'm a coward and I'm a fool, but I'm going to do it anyway.

I'm going to do it anyway because it is my responsibility, Luddie.

It is my responsibility to tell you, Luddie, your country is a tomb.

Your country is a tomb, and it is my responsibility to tell you in a letter even though your tomb is already stuffed with letters.

A tomb is a box of letters stuffed dead, so what's one more?

What's one more letter to you, Luddie, even though I know you are dead?

"She's dead, isn't she," I say to Bernadette in our room, after we return to Krakow.

"Yes," Bernadette says and bursts into tears, "the man in the green wool suit told me. I couldn't say it."

"It's okay," I tell her, "It's not for you to say."

It's not for Bernadette to say, Luddie, it's for me to say, because I brought us here.

I brought us here to this tomb, which is your country.

I brought us here to this tomb, which is your country, where the dead surround the living until finally the dead overwhelm.

The dead overwhelm and engulf the living. They slide the living into the silent tomb of your country.

I have to tell you even though you died years ago.

The man in the green wool suit told Bernadette.

You died years ago in Trzebownisku, and we were never going to find you.

We were never going to give you these letters.

You had no babies.

You were never going to write back.

So what do we do for one another now that we know we'll never correspond, that we'll never see one another, that we'll never touch?

What do we do, Luddie?

It is foolish to write a letter to a dead woman, and I am a fool writing a letter to you in the center of a tomb as an epilogue to a series of echoes.

I am writing a letter to you as an epitaph for a ghost.

I am writing to you to tell you what happens to the living wandering through your country as ghosts, free of touch, correspondence, and witness.

I am writing what happens to the living in your country, and what happens is that the living put the Bombardier to bed, Luddie, and he gives the living a handful of currency before closing the heavy wooden door to his room.

"Here," he says, and "here" he says again, handing me the old escape map.

"I'm sorry," he says, "good night."

"Good night," I say, and Bernadette and I flee into the night to drink with his money and forget his memories, and here we are.

Here we are in a bar in the old Jewish district of Krakow, with its young Polish men and women laughing and drinking.

They all have beautiful faces, Luddie.

They smell great.

We watch the curtains wave into the windows with the night breeze, and we drink with the beautiful faces and the great smells in your tomb. We witness nothing. We correspond with nothing.

Nostrovia, Luddie.

A drink to the dead.

Dear Luddie,

In the morning, we are alive.

In the morning Bernadette, the Bombardier, and I are alive in the light of day, but you are dark, lost in the night, dead, still.

You are dead, and the dugout is gone, and we're alive, showering, brushing our teeth, dressing for a trip back to Berlin without you.

I had wanted so badly to meet you, Luddie.

The Bombardier has your photograph, and we have his map, and these things will have to be enough.

These things will have to be enough, so I touch the map spread out on Bernadette's luggage, and I imagine it could be your shirt.

I imagine it could be your shirt on your arm in Poland. I imagine it could be your shirt, and I daydream you are old, Luddie, but you are alive, smiling at me as I touch your arm in this shirt.

I daydream you have so many stories.

You have so many stories, and you can tell them to me, but the daydream can't last because the dead skin on my fingers catches on the silk of the map as I run my dreamy hand over it.

The dead skin on my fingers pulls the map from the luggage, and I have to stop it from sliding onto the floor.

It's nothing.

I catch the map in my hands and look at it with my bleary eyes.

On the map, I see the Oder River.

I see Blechhammer North.

I see Blechhammer South.

I see Koźle.

Luddie, I look at the map in my hands and I see Koźle, where the death heads of Oświęcim were.

I look at the map in my hands and I see the Oder River, and I see

Blechhammer North, and I see Blechhammer South, but I don't see Brzeg, and I don't see Opole.

I look at the map and I see a black line running from just outside Gleiwitz to Blechhammer North and Blechhammer South near Koźle, and who am I going to tell, Luddie?

Who am I going to tell that I see these things on this map in my hands?

Bernadette is awake, showering and dreading the drive back to Berlin.

The Bombardier is downstairs having breakfast.

I am here with this map in my hands, and who am I going to tell that I can see from this map that we have been wrong?

Who am I going to tell that we didn't see Blechhammer when we drove through Brzeg?

Who am I going to tell that the Bombardier's memory is wrong and his map is right?

Who am I going to tell?

I'm going to tell you, Luddie.

I'm going to tell you even though you are dead because I love you, Luddie, and even the dead, if they are loved, must be told what happens.

I'm going to tell you I run from our room with the map in my hands, Luddie.

I run from our room down to the dining room in our hotel with the map in my hand to show the Bombardier, who is showered, shaved, in his suit, sitting ramrod straight, eating a hard-boiled egg, alive.

Dear Luddie,

We didn't find you because you are dead, but we didn't find Blechhammer because we forget.

We forget what happens to us even a night before, let alone sixty years of nights before.

We forget. Let alone.

We forget where we opened the bomb-bay doors.

We forget at what angle the flames reached us.

We forget the shiny thimble-sized vats we saw from the sky.

We forget the towns we crashed into. We forget the names.

We forget the names on our mother's side, and we forget the towns where these names grew up. We forget the towns and their names and their smells. We forget the diesel and fish and cigarettes, and we forget the cold wool of our first coats.

We forget until the flames of a dishtowel on the stove reach us at a certain angle. We forget until we dream of diesel and fish.

We forget until a woman walks by us with a coat covered in snow and a cigarette in her white hand, and we remember.

We remember sixty years later when our grandson puts an old silk map in front of us and then, at breakfast, after we've learned of a friend's final forgetting, we remember.

We remember Gleiwitz.

We remember Koźle.

We remember Blechhammer, and we run to the samochódy with our maps, our grandsons, and our lovers, and we ride out away from forgetting toward the real remembered Blechhammer with yellow ropes pulling our stomachs and hearts out of the tomb.

Dear Luddie,

The Bombardier says, "Doggone it."

The Bombardier says, "Doggone it," and then he says, "Why did I think the damned I.P. was near Opole?"

He rubs his chin.

We're in the samochódy, riding back where we came from just a few days before, but this time Bernadette is looking at the new map and the old map.

This time we're not trusting the Bombardier's memory.

"Did you bomb anything else around here?" I ask, careening past little junk cars on the highway.

"No," he says, "I must have just not remembered correctly."

He puts the stem of his glasses in his mouth.

"The I.P. *was* Gleiwitz, doggone it," he says, waving his glasses in the air. "Why did I think it was Opole?"

He slaps his hand on my headrest.

"So what did we see near Brzeg?" I ask, ducking forward.

"Damned if I know," he says angrily.

The escape map is in Bernadette's hands.

The escape map is full of clusters of penciled zs and dark grease arrows.

Bernadette points at a cluster of thick zs around Opole and Wroclaw.

"A lot of flack," the Bombardier says, peering up into the front seat. "Gleiwitz, right there. It's the I.P. And the targets, Blechhammer North and Blechhammer South, are very clearly near Koźle."

"So Blechhammer North and South," I say, "must have been on the map at Oświęcim."

The Bombardier says nothing.

"The death's heads?" I say.

256

"Doggone it," says the Bombardier. "I even redrew that arrow on the map for this trip, but I had not thought to look at it. I didn't remember it right."

I laugh.

Bernadette laughs.

The Bombardier almost laughs.

"We can get there today," he says, "but we don't really have more than an hour we can spend if we want to keep to our schedule."

"We'll just see what we see," I say.

We ride along in silence for an hour or so.

The winter is over, but the spring hasn't quite come. The snow has melted into the mud, and all the dull winter colors have begun to bleed.

The day is bright in patches, but I can see a few dark clouds hovering up north.

I steer the samochódy down the bumpy two-lane road Bernadette has found by comparing the Bombardier's old escape map with the new road map.

All around us, silver puddles sit in the ditches and grassy depressions.

The bumpy two-lane road on the new map runs west through to Gleiwitz, the I.P., and then it veers off to where Blechhammer North is on the old escape map, but where nothing is now on the new road map.

I drive, careening past little junk cars and silvery puddles.

"I remember," the Bombardier, says as we approach Gleiwitz, "we had to do a twenty-five-degree turn once we got here to the I.P."

He demonstrates this turn with his hand flat in front of him, then banked.

"We had a 325-degree axis of attack," he says.

The straight lines of the scrubby pine trees blur past either side of us as we turn at Gleiwitz, and I began to feel woolly black clouds spilling

257

from the folds in my brain.

"We would have opened the bomb-bay doors just here," the Bombardier says, looking up into the sky.

The sky is less clear now. It is filling with woolly black clouds.

"As you know," the Bombardier says, looking out the window, "this is the town Hitler invaded in 1939 to start the war."

Bernadette and I do not know, but nod our cloudy heads.

"Poland had a non-aggression pact with Britain and France," the Bombardier says, locking his hands in front of him, "so when the Germans invaded here at Gleiwitz, the Poles asked Britain and France to come to their aid. Of course Britain and France tried to renege, but after three days Britain and France both committed their troops honorably. So it really is here at Gleiwitz that the war began in Europe."

Bernadette holds both maps close to her face.

"This is probably the exact route you flew," she says.

"This is where I opened the bomb-bay doors," he says.

We all fall silent as we drive along this exact route the Bombardier flew.

We all fall silent as we drive along this exact route where sixty years before, the bomb-bay doors opened.

The road, which up until now has been straight, begins to turn as we approach where Blechhammer North should be.

I grip the steering wheel tight.

The scrubby pine trees on both sides of the road begin to look wild and unruly, flashing by too fast, I think.

"What are we looking for?" I ask Bernadette.

She looks down at her maps.

"I'm not sure," she says.

Three emergency vehicles with sirens blaring round a turn in front of us and fly past in the oncoming lane.

My knuckles are white with pink lines.

The black clouds have spread from the horizon to the sky above us and finally into my chest. I feel a surge of panic rise through these clouds.

Are there ghosts in these trees, Luddie? Are you here?

We turn again.

Bernadette says, looking up from the two maps in her lap, "It should be somewhere on our right."

The ghosts and the trees bleed together on our right, Luddie.

On our right, a little further, the ghosts and trees bleed together, and then they break.

On our right, the ghosts and trees break open, and we see crumbling brick walls and jutting iron scaffolds and a broken concrete tower standing in the weeds.

I slam on the brakes, and we screech on the wet pavement.

It has begun to rain. Wet splashes soak the pavement, the samochódy, and the crumbling brick and jutting iron and broken concrete resting in the weeds here in your country. Bombed. Soaked. We all run into the weeds to touch it. The Bombardier, laughing, says, "Do you see it? Do you see it?"

We do, Luddie. We see it.

COLOPHON

Off We Go Into the Wild Blue Yonder was designed at Coffee House Press, in the historic Grain Belt Brewery's Bottling House near downtown Minneapolis. The text is set in Garamond.

FUNDER ACKNOWLEDGMENTS

Coffee House Press receives major operating support from the Bush Foundation, the McKnight Foundation, from Target, and from the Minnesota State Arts Board, through an appropriation by the Minnesota State Legislature and from the National Endowment for the Arts. We have received project support from the National Endowment for the Arts, a federal agency; the Jerome Foundation; and the National Poetry Series. Coffee House also receives support from: three anonymous donors; Abraham Associates; the Elmer L. and Eleanor J. Andersen Foundation; Allan Appel; Around Town Literary Media Guides; Bill Berkson; the James L. and Nancy J. Bildner Foundation; the Patrick and Aimee Butler Family Foundation; the Buuck Family Foundation; Dorsey & Whitney, LLP; Fredrikson & Byron, P.A.; Jennifer Haugh; Anselm Hollo and Jane Dalrymple-Hollo; Jeffrey Hom; Stephen and Isabel Keating; Robert and Margaret Kinney; the Kenneth Koch Literary Estate; Allan & Cinda Kornblum; Seymour Kornblum and Gerry Lauter; the Lenfestey Family Foundation; Ethan J. Litman; Mary McDermid; Rebecca Rand; Debby Reynolds; Schwegman, Lundberg, Woessner, P.A.; Charles Steffey and Suzannah Martin; John Sjoberg; Jeffrey Sugerman; Stu Wilson and Mel Barker; the Archie D. & Bertha H. Walker Foundation; the Woessner Freeman Family Foundation in memory of David Hilton; and many other generous individual donors.

This activity is made possible in part by a grant from the Minnesota State Arts Board, through an appropriation by the Minnesota State Legislature and a grant from the National Endowment for the Arts.

NATIONAL ENDOWMENT FOR THE ARTS

MINNESOTA STATE ARTS BOARD

TARGET.

To you and our many readers across the country, we send our thanks for your continuing support.

Good books are brewing at www.coffeehousepress.org